Bruce Dickson

SINK THE ARK ROYAL

by

Duncan Harding

THUNDERCHILD PUBLISHING
Huntsville, Alabama

This book is a work of fiction. Any references to historical events, real people, or real places are used fictitiously. Other names, characters, places, and events are products of the author's imagination, and any resemblance to actual events or places or persons, living or dead, is entirely coincidental.

SINK THE ARK ROYAL

Published by arrangement with the Charles Whiting literary estate.

ISBN-13: 978-1721293438
ISBN-10: 1721293434

Published by Thunderchild Publishing. Find us at https://ourworlds.net/thunderchild_cms/

Part One

The Draft

Chapter One

"Come on ... come on, chaps ... Shoot the bugger out of the sky ... You're nearly there now!"

Excitedly the naval officers, peering through their binoculars and telescopes at the great ship battling gamely through the heavy seas, fighting desperately to get to the safety of the port before her luck ran out completely, shouted above the crazy pulsating of the guns and the roar of the enemy planes coming in for the stroke of death.

HMS *Ark Royal* was perhaps just over half a mile from the English shore, where motor torpedo-boats and tugs were being hastily scrambled to move out and rescue her. She was going at only half her normal speed, which was not surprising, for she listed heavily to port. Flames were licking hungrily across her flight deck and white smoke was pouring from her aft in a thick, sinister cloud, indicating to the tense watching officers on shore that she had been badly hit in the boilers by the German bombs.

Still she staggered on, breasting the huge, white waves seemingly greedy to drag her down to her death, while the last of the attacking Ju 88s came in for the death blow.

On the sides of the battle-littered flight-deck of the great aircraft carrier, the last of her planes blazing fiercely to aft, the weary gunners prepared to take up the last challenge. *Ark Royal* had been fighting a running battle against the German E-boats, U-boats and aircraft ever since that final run for home on 27 September 1939. Time and time again the German attackers had struck. Now the exhausted gunners beneath their flak-helmets were surrounded by piles of empty shell-cases — and the tarpaulin-covered dead of the last attack were sprawled out in the grotesque, obscene angles of those who had met a violent death.

The twin-engined Ju 88, still out of range though the deadly 'fish' was clearly visible under its blue-painted belly, started to lower its undercarriage. The waiting gunners, tense and sweating behind their pom-poms, 'Chicago pianos' and quick-firers, felt a cold finger of fear trace its way slowly down their backs. They recognised the tactic. The German pilot was a brave man. He was risking being blown out of the air by using the wind resistance of his undercarriage to slow the aircraft down so that his aim with the torpedo would be accurate. But what might well be suicide for that unknown Jerry, they told themselves, could also be the end for them too.

The seconds passed leadenly. On shore, the watching staff officers had ceased shouting encouragement. The situation was too nail-biting, too tense. Grimly, almost hypnotically, they stared through their glasses as the Ju, skidding across the glistening calibrated circles of the optics, came in noisily for the kill. At that moment of high drama, it seemed to the onlookers that there was no escape for the *Ark Royal.* She had come through so many battles in her three years of war: time and time again the Germans had announced they had sunk her. But this time it would be no lie. This time, *Ark Royal* was for the chop!

Now, the distance between the trapped victim and her intended killer lessened by the instant. Staring at the Ju, the watchers could see the white blobs of the faces of the two-man crew under their leather helmets as they prepared to launch that last devastating blow. Here and there an officer cursed, muttering "Damn and blast it, it isn't fair! After all she's been through!" But for the most part the watchers maintained a tense, heart-stopping silence as they waited for the inevitable.

Slowly the release mechanism beneath the Ju started to creak into life. The torpedo, with its ton of deadly explosive, was armed and ready to be launched. There would be no saving *Ark Royal* now; her fate was sealed. A commander among the watchers started to mutter the Lord's Prayer, as if he hoped it might help.

Then, suddenly, the twin-engined torpedo-bomber shuddered violently. On shore, the commander broke off his recitation of the

Lord's Prayer — "Christ Almighty!" he cried in shocked alarm. "She's dropped her bloody egg! There goes the tin fish —"

He stopped short. Suddenly, a lithe, deadly shape had dropped out of the clouds above *Ark Royal* and her attacker. Someone yelled, "Oh, no! ... It can't be ... *it's the bloody Brylcreem boys!"*

It was. At 400 mph, zooming in at sea level, its prop-wash lashing the waves below it into a white, boiling fury, the Spitfire came racing after the unsuspecting Ju, eight Browning machine-guns already blazing fire. Lethally, the white-and-red tracer zipped across the intervening distance in a deadly stream.

Pieces of metal began to flutter from the torpedo-bomber. The plane faltered in mid-air, seeming to stop for a moment, as if it had just run into a wall. Then the German aircraft, white glycol spurting from its port engine, rallied. Desperately the pilot tried to keep the aircraft airborne as the angry slugs ripped the length of its fuselage. Now the port engine was fully aflame, the fire was beginning to spread along the wing. The paint began to bubble and erupt like the symptoms of a loathsome skin disease. The Ju was dying in mid-air.

"Knock the fucker out of the sky ... knock her out!" screamed the commander who had recited the Lord's Prayer. Then he stopped in mid-sentence. The dying Ju had lurched violently as the torpedo dropped from beneath its belly. For a moment, relieved of the ton weight the dive-bomber sprang upward. *"Hell's bells and little fishes!"* one of the watchers yelled miserably. *"She's launched her tin fish. Oh, my friggin' sainted aunt!"*

What happened next was seared into the minds of those watchers who survived the war. In the same instant that the torpedo's electric motor was activated and in a flurry of exploding bubbles of compressed air the weapon started for its target, the German aircraft fell out of the sky. It hit the sea, bounced high once and then went under in a huge eruption of boiling water. It was then that the Spitfire pilot acted. He saw the danger as the torpedo raced for the helpless *Ark Royal,* wallowing in the shallow water, her gunners unable to depress their weapons in order to knock out the tin fish before destruction overtook them. The Spitfire raced forward at full throttle, heading straight for the crippled aircraft carrier. Standing by a burning Gladiator on the flight-deck, a bare-headed petty officer waved angrily at the approaching British fighter, as if he were trying to swat a fly. But the pilot kept on course doggedly, his keen eyes scanning the shallow sea. There — there it was!

"Tally ho!" he yelled in triumph and pushed the joystick forward. The fighter dropped even lower and he could feel the presence of the sea close to him, trying to drag his plane under. Going all-out, every bolt and rivet squealing in protest at the pressure, feeling as if his aircraft might disintegrate at any moment, the unknown pilot raced after the torpedo as it hurtled forward on its course of death and destruction.

Suddenly the pilot opened fire. Below, the surface of the sea was whipped into a white fury, lashed by the mad hail of bullets. The pilot saw the torpedo shudder — he had hit it, but he didn't wait to see what happened next and frantically jerked the stick back. The Spitfire's sharp nose tilted upwards. For one awful moment he thought the old kite wouldn't respond. *"Christ!"* he yelled to himself, *"She's going to stall, the bitch!"* But his aircraft didn't, instead the Merlin engine took the strain and in a moment he was hurtling upward. In that same instant the torpedo exploded harmlessly in a great blinding flash and bedlam of noise that seemed to last forever. Majestically, the battered *Ark Royal* limped through the crazy, heaving sea, heading for Pompey and safety.

A mile high in the grey sky, the pilot of the four-engined German Focke-Wulf, which had shadowed the aircraft-carrier ever since they had first spotted her in the Bay of Biscay and the battle had commenced, whooped with joy. *"Hein!"* he pressed his throat-mike and chortled to the second-pilot by his side. "We've stuck that fish right up the arse of the *Ark Royal!"* He emphasised the name gleefully. "The pride of the Tommy navy has been sunk at shitting last!" Carried away by excitement, he clicked on the radio which linked him to his home base.

"Maria Olga Dora here," he snapped urgently. "Do you read me, Control? Maria Olga Dora here ... do you read me ...!"

Control Lorient answered immediately. Crackling and distorted, the disembodied, metallic voice said, "Read you, M-O-D ... loud and clear. Report ... over."

The *Luftwaffe* pilot suppressed his excitement the best he could, the sight of that great explosion far below still filling his mind's eye. Hastily he passed on the tremendous news. *"What — what did you say, M-O-D?"* the metallic voice at base gasped incredulously.

"Tell the boys of *Geschwader Funfzig",* the German pilot rasped after he had repeated his news, "that there'll be a wing-dinger tonight and it'll be paid for by no less a person than the Gift Dwarf.* Real champers — none of that German sparkling wine muck. And women, too. Tell 'em to empty that big whorehouse on the Rue Port reserved for field officers and upwards. No poxy whore this night. The Gift Dwarf, you can be sure when he hears this great news, will have pockets that'll never empty. He's been trying to sink that Tommy ship since war broke out. Now she's finally sunk, and he'd better cough up. For once, the little club-footed bastard can really tell the truth. Over."

But at the other end there was no resumption of standard wireless procedure. Instead, the dazed, disembodied voice of Control said, as if the speaker could not believe his own ears. *"Erdlich ... at last ... We've sunk the shitty* Ark Royal *at shitting last. WE'VE GOT HER ...!"*

* Josef Goebels, under-sized Minister of Public Enlightenment and Propaganda.

Chapter Two

That final explosion of the German torpedo half a mile away slopped greasy, scummy, grey water over the side of the tin bath in front of the coke fire and splashed it onto the *Daily Mirror* beside the bath.

Drake cursed dourly and said for the benefit of his long-suffering wife in the flowered pinafore, who hovered about him as she usually did during his weekly bath, "Bloke can't get his friggin' bath in peace these days!" The grizzled old petty officer, with his skinny white chest gnarled by the battle scars he had gained in the 'Old War', as he called it, handed the face-cloth to his wife. "Here yer are, Maggie, wash me back down, luv, will yer!"

She looked doubtful and pushed back the steel curler which threatened to edge its way from beneath the turban she wore. "A bit cold for washing yer back," she commented. "Catch yer death."

He looked up at her, showing the tombstones of his big yellow false teeth. "Cold water never did nobody any harm," he answered. "Good for yer sex life. Gets the old John Thomas working, cold water does!"

Reluctantly she took the cloth and dipped it into the scummy water of the tin bath. "You and yer John Thomas," she said scornfully. "The times you've dipped yer wick it should have fallen off by now!"

Drake grinned naughtily and reached out his skinny claw to grab her left breast, but she pulled back swiftly. "Now watch yersen, Duggie Drake," she said. "You've had yer day, yer know. Ought to be ashamed of yersen!"

His grin broadened. "That's what you think, Maggie, with me soon to go to sea agen and all. I've got to get me cards punched a few times more. I'm not gonna go off and leave it all to that fancy man o' yours!"

She frowned. "There's no fancy man, Duggie Drake, and well you know it. Besides, what do you want to go to sea agen at your age? You've done yer bit, haven't yer — and then some." Her eyes flooded with tears.

He recognised the signs. He had seen them many times before in all the years they had been married. "Don't be a daft old tart," he said without rancour. "Do me back and then get the 'Wintergreen'," meaning the hot plaster which he had worn for years now ever since the effects of being twelve hours in the freezing sea when his ship had been sunk at the Battle of Jutland. Since then his back had hurt badly.

Maggie washed his back, then dried it and her hands before rising to pick up the plaster from the dresser, underneath the fading picture of the 10th Cruiser Squadron off Shanghai back in the 1920s. She looked at the ships, all gleaming brass, polish and scrubbed woodwork, and he said as he reached for his knee bandages, "Aye, them was the days. I was full of piss and vinegar then. Not a bloody old cripple of a sailorman like I am now, who would have been beached long ago if it hadn't been for this war."

"You're not old, Duggie," she said dutifully, trying to get her thumbnail under the edge of the plaster. "Just a bit stiff."

He began to bind the thick bandages round his crippled knees, saying, "Aye, stiff, only I don't get stiff in the right place, if yer know what I mean, Maggie, old lass."

"I know what yer mean, yer old goat," she answered warily. Over at the port the matelots were cheering, the sirens were shrieking and hands were being clapped loudly. Wise in the ways of the Royal Navy as she was, Maggie told herself that some other desperate ship had made it back to harbour, probably half wrecked like so many of them were these days, with the dead matelots wrapped in canvas and stretched out in stiff lines on the aft deck. She shook her old head and tried again with the plaster.

"Is it proper 'Wintergreen?'" Drake asked, finishing bandaging his knobbly knees. "Don't want no imitation rubbish. Lot of that about these days."

"Jones the Chemist," she answered, at last getting started on the plaster, "said this one would burn the balls off'n a bull. It'll toast yer friggin' kidneys till hell freezes over!"

CPO Drake's jaw dropped. "What did yer say? Jones the Chemist wouldn't say nothin' like that, would he?"

"Course not, yer silly old sod," she snorted. "But don't think you're the only one around here who can use bad language. Now then — brace yersen!"

He bent his skinny back and he was that thin she could count his ribs. "Go on, bung the bugger on. Give us a treat, yer mother's drunk."

She did so, smoothing the plaster, smelling of menthol and other aromatics, while he writhed and shivered, muttering, "It's bloody cold. Give me my shirt, love."

She shook her head in mock wonder. "Yer can tell you was one of the toffs, Duggie Drake, brought up in a manor house with hot and cold running servants." She handed him the fresh shirt. "What would you do without me, I wonder?"

By way of an answer he rose stiffly and advanced upon her, moving like an old man due to the tight crepe bandages wrapped round his knees. They and the plaster were the only things that seemed to keep his rheumatic pains at bay when he was at sea and exposed to the freezing cold for hours on end. With surprising tenderness for such a hard man he enfolded her in his skinny arms, saying, "I don't know, Maggie. You're the one, aren't you! You know that, lass. Now what do you think if we have a little tot before it all starts agen and ends, well, God knows where?"

His sunken-cheeked, leathery face looked so old and vulnerable at that moment that tears suddenly blinded her eyes. For an instant she had a moment of total recall, as she remembered him coming back just after the 'Old War'. He had swaggered into the smoky, noisy waterfront pub as if he owned it. His cap was shoved to the back of his curly head, his broad chest was ablaze with new medal ribbons and his even white teeth gleamed like an ad for

Gibbs' toothpaste. "Full of wind and piss" he was, as he had described himself years later. "God's gift to womankind!"

What a handsome, devil-may-care young man he had been all those years ago, Maggie told herself. Now his chest was sunken, the sparse hairs which adorned it were white and those current shiny yellow teeth had come from the Hassler, the naval hospital at Portsmouth. Protectively, her eyes brimming with tears of pity and regret, she pressed his skinny frame to her ample, motherly body.

"Now then, Chiefie," she heard herself saying, attempting to be jolly. "Whoever heard of anyone having a rum at this time of the morning? You've a long day before yer till they tell yer your posting. You'll need all yer strength to keep from sitting down on the job."

He pulled himself away, the drink abruptly forgotten. He realised that she was talking sense, as usual. He wanted a posting. He'd been on the beach too long, shuffling bits of paper about from one frigging office to another. He needed sea-going duty. Who knows, it might be the last sea-tour he'd get before they gave him the chop on account of old age. Blokes pushing sixty were not too welcome in the Royal, even if there was a shortage of bodies.

"All right, old lass. You've got the last word as ruddy always. Sling us me cap and gasmask." As she did so, the sirens started to wail along the coast, sounding their customary warning. "Bloody friggin' Jerries!" he muttered routinely under his breath. "Never give yer a moment's friggin' peace."

"It's one of them new tip-and-run raiders," Maggie suggested. She meant the amazingly fast Focke-Wulf 190 fighter-bombers which had replaced the more ponderous bomber squadrons of the previous year. The FW 190s came in fast and low, dropped their 1,000 lb bomb load on some coastal road or resort before skimming back to their French bases at very low altitude to avoid British radar.

"Aye," Duggie agreed as he placed his cap carefully on his thinning hair, trying to get it at the regulation angle. He had no truck with those cocky Hostilities Only chappies, serving in the war years only, who poised their caps right at the back of their heads to show off their carefully combed locks, usually longer than regulation length.

He pressed her to him once more before he stepped out of their small terraced house straight into the street, looking every inch the chief petty officer with thirty years service, who feared neither God nor man.

In a passing train, Sub-Lieutenant Guy de Gray looked up abruptly as the first bomb struck the ground 200 yards away. He was just in time to catch a glimpse of an elderly petty officer kissing a plump woman in curlers before he disappeared beyond the windows of the little terraced house below the railway line. The train shuddered and, opposite him, the fat businessman with the tortoiseshell glasses, who had the self-satisfied look of a black marketeer, said indignantly, "Can't think what the boys in blue are doing to allow the Jerries to bomb us like this and get away with it."

He puffed hard until his fat jowls wobbled. "What are we paying our taxes for, eh?" He looked challengingly at the handsome young naval officer, clearly just commissioned; his greatcoat was too new and his cap was still stiff and not yet battered like most officers' caps were.

Guy de Gray coloured for no reason apparent to him. But then he always flushed when people spoke to him. It was something he did automatically when he was addressed by senior officers, even elderly CPOs and — above all — girls, from Wrens with faces like sour lemons to teenage shopgirls outside the local Palais de Danse, who were all too obviously to be 'had' for a port-and-lemon and a fish supper.

De Gray jerked a thumb at a fading picture in the first-class compartment they shared, encouraging the pre-war holiday-maker to enjoy a 'break at bracing Bognor!' Beneath it some official had stuck the current slogan urging 'Careless Talk Costs Lives'.

The fat civilian chuckled knowingly. "Don't kid yersen, Lieutenant," he said. "The average street-tart in Pompey knows everything that's going on hereabouts. And if they know it, you can bet yer bottom dollar that old Jerry knows it as well!" He started visibly as nearby another bomb shattered the morning calm. De Gray did so too and again he flushed, as if it were his fault. "They'll soon know about where them bombs dropped and what ship it is that's coming into port." The fat man pointed to the great grey giant, listing badly, black smoke pouring from below her decks, as the tugs started to throw up their lines in order to haul her into harbour.

De Gray shuddered. He already knew the name of that wounded giant. It was the legendary *Ark Royal,* which, according to their propaganda, the Jerries had sunk a dozen times since the outbreak of war in September 1939. Now the gallant aircraft carrier had apparently done it again.

The fat businessman didn't appear to notice the young officer's surprise. Instead, he said: "Talking about tarts and the like ..." he licked his full, sensual lips and there was a new light behind the thick lenses of his glasses. "Young feller like yersen might need something to — er — help him with the Judies. They're a fussy lot in Pompey, yer know — too many matelots and too few tarts." He looked swiftly from left to right as if he felt he might be observed and snapped open the brown attaché-case on his lap. "Knicks!" he drooled. "Stuff like you ain't seen since before the war. Gay Paree, ooh, la-de-la sort of thing. Just the stuff to give the troops!"

De Gray looked worried as the fat man dipped into the case with both hands and brought out a pair of sheer black panties, stretching the material apart with his thumbs, and he thrust them at De Gray, babbling, "Come on! Just look at 'em! Fancy having a bit of the other in them as well!" He licked his fat lips. "A bloke could die happy after that, couldn't he!"

As usual, the young naval office blushed a furious red.

"Now, sir," the fat man snapped, this time very businesslike, for the train was beginning to slow down as it entered Portsmouth's bombed main station. "What's it going to be for the little lady tonight? This, or this darling little number?" Deftly, like a magician producing a rabbit from a hat, he dived again into the case and brought out a pair of skimpy red silk knickers, which when he held them up proved to have no crotch. "Quick release we call this in the trade!" he said, winking knowingly at the scarlet-faced youth. "Especially if yer hasty young Lothario has only got a wall to perform against, if yer follow my meaning, sir." He winked again and de Gray wanted the carriage floor to open up and swallow him. In a few seconds passengers would be filing by and they only needed to glance to their right and see ... He daren't even *think* that embarrassing thought to its logical conclusion.

"Now, sir. What's your decision? Which of these delightful knicks do you want!" He leered at the red-faced young officer. "Make your choice now. Thirty bob a pair. By this time tomorrow they'll be all gone. They'll be snatching them out of my h —"

He never finished. Gut de Gray gave a barely suppressed sigh of relief as a self-important RTO officer with his brassard and clip-board came down the corridor, rapping on the compartment windows with his pencil and snapping, "All new drafts to Portsmouth report immediately to the Railway Transport Office ... all new drafts ..."

Hastily, the young sub-lieutenant grabbed his case and cap from the net above his head, murmured something to the fat man, still holding out the crotchless knickers, and got off the train.

Moments later he was submerged in the wartime hustle and bustle of a mainline station, where keen-eyed shore patrols of petty officers kept watch for deserters. Whores in cheap flowery dresses lurked in the shadows looking for customers; officials, military and civilian showed off their importance, and everywhere streams of jaunty, defiant, pale-faced matelots with kitbags slung over their shoulders pushed their way to the blue-painted buses which would take them to the barracks and their own personal date with destiny.

Chapter Three

"Schau her, der geile Beck," the studio electrician murmured enviously to his workmate, "Off he goes again, the randy goat. He'll be up the skirts of one of them new starlets before this take is over, mark my words, Rudi!"

Next to him, Rudi, the sound-man, spat out his cigarette-end and sourly nodded his agreement as he watched the little man with his sharp, cynical dark eyes and monstrous club-foot hurry through the scenery towards the junior UFA stars' dressing-cabins. "Don't know how the damn cripple does it," he said, "with that foot and the little bit of dried-up gristle he must have between his skinny shanks."

Hans-Peter, his old friend and workmate, made the Continental gesture of counting money and added, "Yer know them so-called stars. They'd suck the cock of the friggin' studio dog if it could promise them a nice juicy part in the next UFA film. Morals of an alley-cat, all them pretty tarts — and the way they play them innocent country girls in those crappy *Heimatfilme** you'd think butter wouldn't melt in their dirty, sexy mouths."

"Yes, if you happen to have the right ration card to get the friggin' butter, Hans-Peter."

The other technician laughed hollowly. "Golden pheasants" — he meant Nazi Party officials — "can get anything they shitting-well like," and with that said he went back to work underneath the large red poster which read, 'Our Fuhrer knows only battle and worry, let us take part of that from him'. He sighed and told himself — he daren't say the words aloud, even to his workmate — "I know

* German rural films.

what piece of him I'd take off!"

Dr Goebbels, his sallow, cynical face flushed a little both with the effort of walking fast and excitement, paused behind the mass of lights, dollies and the usual clutter of the Babelsberg's 'film factory', as it was called, and threw a glance over his skinny shoulder. There was no one. He had thrown off his usual entourage, the two hulking Gestapo men who kept tabs on his behaviour for the Fuhrer, and his own bodyguard, a large ex-boxer, needed to ward off angry husbands and lovers. He smiled thinly. This was his chance. Unconsciously, he echoed the words of the disgruntled stage-hand. "I can do anything I want," he said aloud and then, tucking at the white dust-coat that reached to his ankles and which he thought hid his deformity to some extent, he started to limp towards the twins, 'Toby and Toxi's' dressing-room.

They might well only be fifteen, well below the legal age, he told himself, drooling a little in anticipation. But from the looks they had just flashed to him back on the sound-stage (where they were playing small parts in one of the usual circus movies that the 'mob', as he called the cinema audience, seemed to like) they knew what it was all about. The way they had contorted their lithe young, half-naked bodies on the high-wire had been done specially for him, he knew that. And if they made a fuss afterwards, as sometimes one or two of his 'pigeons' (as he called them) did, they'd soon be dealt with. There was always 'sugar and the whip', he told himself gleefully as he turned into the dark corridor of wooden boxes which belonged to the 'stars of the future', as they proclaimed themselves to be. "That's the way to treat a woman — *sugar and the whip.*"

He limped down the alley to the box from which he could hear the sound of girlish laughter and silly chatter. They were there all right. He stopped and standing on his toes with difficulty he peered inside through the little window. The Star Dressing-room was filled with the usual clutter of such places — wigs on heads, spangled dresses thrown over screens, a dressing-table lit by coloured lights, tins and bottles of cosmetics, and on the floor, carelessly dropped in their haste to change for the next take, delightful wisps of transparent underwear.

At this moment, however, his eyes were not on the interior but on the two figures in the centre of the box. The two girls were totally naked and unabashed, as Toxi (at least he thought it was Toxi) carefully powered the beautifully shaped back of her sister, her tiny, pink-tipped virginal breasts quivering slightly with her movements.

Goebbels swallowed hard and felt the old, familiar stirrings in his loins. He ran his greedy gaze down Toxi's athlete's body from her small breasts down to her beautiful flat stomach, and that delightful vee of tight, curly pubic hair. She obviously wasn't a true blonde, but although the dark-haired Minister for Propaganda preferred blondes it didn't matter in Toxi's case. For his mind was racing with excitement as he imagined taking the two of them together, blonde or not. He didn't know exactly how, but he had been working in his mind at various combinations, allowing his vivid sexual imagination its full lustful range.

Toxi said something. Dutifully, Toby bent slightly and opened her shapely legs. "My God!" Goebbels muttered to himself, "What legs!" and then his perverted heart almost stopped beating as he caught a glimpse of her vulva and the nest of curly black hair. *"Mei Jo!"* he cursed excitedly in his native Rhenish dialect, "It's so good, I could ... could *eat* it!"

Toxi finished her sister's make-up and before starting on her own she tottered to the dressing-table in her high heels and sat down carelessly to light a cigarette. Then, puffing out the blue smoke languorously, she parted her legs and said something to her sister, one hand dropping down between her thighs.

The watcher could hardly contain himself. His dark face flushed hotly and he felt a vein begin to throb frantically on his left temple. For a moment he wondered if it was all too much for him; whether he was going to have a stroke, brought on by all the excitement. For one long instant he was tempted to throw open the door and fling himself on the shameless Toxi, who seemed to be enjoying whatever she was demonstrating to her sister. Then he contained himself, just in time. If he were to get them to do what he wanted, he would have to remain calm and suave: the great Minister, who stood next in importance to no less a person than the Fuehrer himself.

Goebbels pulled himself together. He smoothed back his long, sleek hair and advanced the last few paces to the dressing-room door. Inside, they were still giggling at something and Toxi was still engaged in lovingly stroking herself between her legs. Trying to be calm, he was bathed in hot sweat at the thought of having the twins. Toxi, for certain, was delightfully perverted for her age — he supposed it was due to being around with film folk. She'd offer no objection to a threesome and she looked as if she would easily convince her sister to go along with this naughty sexual escapade. He raised his hand to knock on the door before entering and enjoying that moment of fake confusion and apparent shock, when they'd be simpering, *"Ach, Herr Minister ... Ein Moment, bitte, wir haben keine Kleider an ... "* and trying at the same time with one pair of hands to cover their young breasts and shadow of pubic hair. But this fine autumn afternoon, the dwarf-like Minister of Public Enlightenment and Propaganda - "Let me enlighten you, my dear. After all, that is my job" — was not fated to enjoy the twins' undoubted charms.

A familiar voice came from somewhere behind him, crying *"Ach, da Sie sind, Herr Reichsminister. Ich habe Sie uberall gesucht."*

"Heaven, arse and cloudburst!" Goebbels cursed angrily and reluctantly let his hand fall from the door. He swung round, face red with rage instead of sexual passion. It was Dr Otto Dietrich, his main assistant; a clever man but lacking all the social graces and savvy. "Dammit, man!" he said softly, as inside the changing-room the giggling had abruptly ceased. "Haven't you got any sense?"

Dietrich's expression changed as it suddenly dawned on him that he had interrupted one of the little *Herr Doktor's* adventures. "Sorry, Herr Minister," he murmured in a crestfallen manner, "but you ordered me to inform you immediately any time that something new came in."

"Came in on what?" Goebbels snapped. He could hear the rustle of silk and organdie as the twins slipped into their stage costumes ready for the next scene.

"The *Ark Royal."*

"What about it? The *Luftwaffe* sunk it, didn't they? We have already filled the papers with the news. There'll be a newsreel in this week's *Deutsche Wochenschen."* Goebbels was referring to the

German cinema newsreel put out by his Ministry. "And that's about the end of the matter, man!"

"No, sir, no it isn't," Dietrich corrected him hesitantly.

"What do you mean?" Goebbels bellowed, suddenly enraged. He had just looked through the window of the little dressing-room and had caught Toxi (or was it Toby?) bending down to adjust a stocking. The gown on its hoop had billowed up at that moment to reveal her delectable, kissable rump, clad only in the sheerest of lace. Now he was going to miss that delightful body — today at least and the thought maddened him.

"Herr Reichsminister," Dietrich chided in a shocked tone. "Your voice — remember your position —"

"Damn my position! Where's the fire?"

"This, sir." He handed the Minister a copy of the British *Daily Mirror,* with its red crusader on the front page. "Look at the date and the picture, It's yesterday's paper, straight from Lisbon this morning."

Goebbels grunted something and stared at the picture and the caption, which read: 'The good old *Ark* does it again. The Admiralty reports that the unsinkable *Ark Royal,* pride of the Royal Navy's Fleet Air Arm, has survived another dastardly Jerry attack ..." He crumpled the paper up and snorted, "Any fool could fake a picture like that, including the hole in the side of her hull. The English are simply engaged in a propaganda exercise until the stink blows over."

For most of the time, Dr Dietrich, with his large horn-rimmed spectacles and his pale, academic's face, was out of place in Dr Goebbels' presence. He was used to the gentler tones of the University of Gottingen from which he had been rudely plucked in 1939. Granted a commission in the *Wehrmacht,* he had become one of the Minister's chief aides because of his almost perfect English. He did not understand Goebbels' quick, cynical mind and, in the middle of total war, his relentless pursuit of women: surely, a German Minister should be concerning himself with matters of national importance, not such trivia as skirt-chasing. But whenever his judgement was challenged, *Herr Professor der Anglistik* Dr Dietrich felt his hackles rise with rage. They did so now, as he said bitingly: "If you don't believe me, Herr Minister, then you might believe the word of the military attachés of the Irish Free State, Switzerland and Spain?"

"All hacks, bought hacks!" Goebbels sneered. "Those so-called neutrals would say anything for this" — and he made a gesture of counting money. "But go on. What do they say?"

"On the day she sailed in, all three were invited to see the damaged *Ark Royal* at the naval base of Portsmouth — and they were invited by Churchill himself."

"Naturally," sneered Goebbels ironically. "Who else?"

But irony was wasted on Dr Dietrich. Doggedly, he continued. "All three attachés reported to their respective embassies and governments that although the aircraft carrier had been badly hit by our bombs she was seaworthy and could soon be at sea again. Naturally their reports were forwarded to us yesterday and this morning."

"Naturally." Again the irony was wasted on the ex-Professor of English.

Dietrich waited while Goebbels considered things, the twins forgotten, at least temporarily. Again he had been thwarted, he told himself, just as he had been by Nature right from the start; he had been given a first-class brain in a cripple's body and that of a dwarf to boot. Right at the beginning of the war he had decided that the British Army was hopelessly antiquated, undersized and no threat to Germany, but the British Navy was something else. With its terrible blockade of the 'turnip winter'* of World War One the Royal Navy had helped to bring Germany to its knees and caused the war-weary revolution on the Home Front which had forced the Kaiser to go into exile.

Then he, Goebbels, had decided he must portray the British fleet as weak and inefficient. The Tommies had played right into his hands and had allowed two of their capital ships to be sunk easily with great loss of life. But that hadn't been sufficient for the crippled dwarf. As he had expounded to his State secretaries at the Berlin Ministry: "Most of the Tommies' capital ships are antiquated, tarted-up veterans of World War One. Ours, thanks to the Fuehrer, are the most modern in the world, but there is one type of craft the Tommies

* The winter of 1919 when Germany survived on turnips.

possess and we do not" — he looked sternly at his high-ranking officials, as if it was their fault — "and that is the aircraft carrier. Ours, the *Graf Zeppelin,* won't be off the stocks until 1950. Now, *meine Herren,"* he had continued, leaning forward to give his listeners the full power of his glittering, dark eyes, "I want their newest aircraft carrier sunk with as much fuss as possible — pictures, the survivors, the lot. The world must know that the German navy, the *Kreigsmarine,* is capable of sinking the most up-to-date ship, the capital ship of the future, making all others obsolete, the British *Ark Royal!"*

Thus had begun the Minister's almost personal feud with the British aircraft carrier, with Goebbels at times clutching at straws, ready to believe the wildest rumours, the craziest 'eyewitness account' by some drink-sodden U-boat skipper, that the *Ark Royal* had gone to the bottom of the sea. Three times he had sunk that damned ship, only to find to his chagrin that the aircraft carrier was still afloat.

More than once, the English traitor in his employ, William Joyce, known to British listeners as 'Lord Haw Haw' because of his upper-class accent, had given full details of a sinking that had not taken place at all, as he had done the previous night from Radio Luxembourg. The whole business was becoming dreadfully embarrassing and Goebbels knew that, behind his back, his fellow Ministers Goering, Himmler and the like, were grinning smugly that he was the only Party member who was capable of sinking a Tommy capital-ship single-handed — *the same one over and over again!*

Dr Goebbels restrained himself with difficulty from making another scene. Up from the sound-stage he could hear the almost military stamp of the big blonde chorus girls in their skimpy shorts, going through their dance routine from the latest movie. From below, where the chorus-master drilled them like some Prussian martinet from the time of Frederick the Great, he knew you could see right up their crotches. The blasé chorus girls, who had all been through the mill long ago, were decidedly careless about wearing knickers under their tight shorts. He licked his lips in anticipation. That sight might be some compensation for the failure of his attempt on the twins' alleged virginity. *"Herr Doktor,"* he said, being as polite as a man with his volatile temper could ever be, "I want you to watch this *Ark Royal* situation. You are to attach yourself to Admiral Raeder's HQ as my personal representative in the matter of that aircraft carrier." Admiral Karl Raeder was chief of the *Kriegsmarine.*

"But I know nothing of such matters," protested the ex-Professor of English. But Goebbels was not listening. His mind's eye was already viewing that long line of delightful crotches. "You have my full authority to use every means possible to get Raeder to sink the *Ark Royal* the next time she leaves port. Money, baubles," he shrugged cynically at the mention of decorations for bravery, "starlets, are all there in plenty in case a bribe is needed. The main thing is, *mein lieber Herr Doktor,"* he emphasised the title maliciously, "that if you wish to avoid being sent to the Russian Front you will ensure that the *Ark Royal* is at the bottom of the ocean before this autumn is over. *Klar?"* Dietrich paled at the threat.

"Klar, Herr Minister," Dietrich answered unhappily.

"Good!" Then Dr Josef Goebbels, Minister for Public Entertainment and Propaganda, was hobbling away to where those juicy crotches awaited him as fast as his deformed foot would carry him.

Chapter Four

"Look lively now, lads!" the Leading Hand, an old red-faced three-striper with the bulbous nose of a hard drinker, said heartily. "Job to be done, war to be won, all that kind of bull!" He grinned at his own humour.

Moaning and complaining, the new draft dropped from the backs of their trucks, grabbed their kitbags and formed a rough-and-ready line in front of the old salt.

"Don't know what he's looking so ruddy happy about," Bunts said out of the side of his mouth to his old running-mate Sparks. "A couple o' years and he'll be looking at the taties from below."

"But I'll make a happy stiff, sailor," the cheerful three-striper, who had caught the remark, responded without rancour. "Short life but a sweet one. I've had more grunt and grumble than you've had hot dinners, laddie!"

"'Grunt and grumble'?"* Bunts queried. Sparks formed a circle with his forefinger and thumb and poked the middle finger of his other hand through the hole. Bunts grinned and nodded. "Got it!"

They marched on, weighed down under their gear, stepping over pipes that ran everywhere, dodging gantry arms, coming to a sudden ragged halt as shunting-engines puffed and rattled across the docks, dragging their cargoes of naval supplies and leaving great streams of choking black smoke behind them. It was the controlled confusion of a naval dockyard working flat out in wartime. But here

*'Grunt and grumble', rhyming slang.

and there they caught glimpses of civilian dockers hidden behind tin sheds, brewing tea over braziers, reading their *Daily Mirrors* and puffing away at stolen cigarettes in happy contentment.

When he spotted the 'skivers', as he called them, the three-striper would command, "At attention now! Swing them arms. Bags of swank now! Remember, you're now the Royal's new elite at a bob a day. New rich, you lot are! Not like yer average dockie struggling to get by on ten quid a week and all he can half-inch from Government stores." In reply, the dockers gave the usual response of two upturned fingers or a contemptuous fart, accompanied by, "Have a ride on that 'un, sailor boy!"

"Cheeky sods!" Sparks moaned. "Ought to get some service in." Once he had been known universally as 'Mick' when he had transferred from the navy of the Irish Free State to that of the British Empire. Since he had obtained his rating as a wireless specialist he had been called 'Sparks' according to tradition. It was the same with his Yorkshire running-mate Bunts, a 'lifer' who was inordinately proud of his rating and the fact that he was one of the fastest signallers in the Navy. "In charge of the signal flags at Trafalgar, I was," he used to boast. "That's how we won the battle, with my smart signalling. But natch, I let old Nelson have the credit, didn't I!" Running-mates as they were, the red-headed, volatile Irishman and the good-hearted Yorkshireman were always, it seemed, at each other's throat. As more than one messmate had said about their constant bickering in the past: 'With friends like that, lads, who needs enemies? What a friggin' pair of oppos!'

They marched for what seemed a long time to naval ratings, who hated walking at the best of times: "Didn't join the old Royal to grow bunions on the old plates o' meat, yer know, mates!" But now they were coming to the far end of the quayside, not far from which large ships, including capital ones, were anchored, in some cases with gangplanks running from ship to ship and along which ratings in dungarees doubled back and forth bearing supplies and equipment. But as interesting as all the capital ships were, all eyes in the new draft were fixed firmly on the great ship anchored in the Sound, a little way off from the rest of the ships, faint wisps of grey smoke still drifting from her interior through shattered, buckled side-plates, one of the few signs that the craft was still manned. The only matelots visible were a deck crew, barefoot and with their dungarees rolled up, who were scrubbing the blackened flight-deck, and a group of officers conferring earnestly, their white caps indicating that they were from some hot climate overseas.

As the draft halted yet again to let another square-boilered nineteenth century shunting engine puff and grunt past, pulling its cargo of wooden store-boxes, the three-striper said: "Yes, I know. I know that you also know what that ship is. But although half of Pompey also knows, keep it under yer friggin' hats. We've got trouble enough. We don't want the friggin' Jerries to start blitzing us agen on account o' her. My old trouble-and-strife is friggin' trouble enough."

They raised a smile and Sparks commented: "Ye could allus run away to sea, Stripey!"

But before the easy-going three-badge man could respond, a tough old voice, heard easily over the clatter of the shunting engine, rasped: "No talking in the ranks! Remember who you are!"

"Christ!" whispered Bunts under his breath, "I forgot that the day I joined up."

For his part, his running-mate Sparks said nothing. Instead, he eyed the tall, skinny, grey-haired Chief Petty Officer who barred his way, hands on hips, staring at them as if they were the lowest form of animal life, which, he told himself, they were. Cannon-fodder for the great battles to come at sea.

The man smiled easily. One could see why he remained a three-badge man after probably a lifetime at sea, including boy's service. He knew his job backwards, but he was clearly too easy-going to be an NCO. He had no desire to 'bear down on the men', as it was called. Now, he said, "What d'yer want done with this little lot, Chiefie?"

CPO Drake looked at the smiling sailor frostily. "For one, to you I'm not *Chiefie,* but *Chief Petty Officer.* And for another thing, that's not the way to report a draft. What d'yer mean, *'this little lot'?* That shower of shit over there, I might point out, are sailors in the Navy of the King Emperor!"

The three-striper wasn't put out. Sparks told himself that the old salt had probably received many bollockings like that ever since he had gained his badge. He took it all in good part, saying, "Correct, Chief Petty Officer. What's the orders, sir?"

Drake relaxed a little and the draft could see by the way he moved slowly and stiffly as he bent his head down to look at his check-board just how old he was. Finally he found what he sought. He commanded, "All right, Draft ... Draft, stand at ease ... Stand Easy!"

There were huge sighs of relief, a few of the usual defiant farts (of which Drake took no notice. He had heard them often enough and took them for what they were — infantile attempts at dumb insolence), and a clatter as the men lowered their kitbags down to the wet quayside, slicked everywhere with oil. He gave them a minute as the dock machinery continued to clatter and the seagulls came racing in, keening like lost children as they dived to where a dirty cook was dumping his ship's swill over the side. "All right, listen to what I've got to say to you. And mark it well because I won't say it again." He paused and his breath fogged in the cold air. "There are several new drafts coming in, including yours. At the moment there is no posting for you." He looked down suddenly at the wet tarmac, as if something in his old eye might reveal the fact that he knew more than he was prepared to tell them at this moment.

"There's at least half-a-dozen ships that are paying off this week and they will be needing new drafts. You'll be one of them, and if you're good boys, who don't pinch the purser's jam and drift away for a quiet spit and draw in the heads when you shouldn't, I'll see you get a nice cushy battlewagon as your billet." He smiled at them, giving them the full benefit of Hassler's false teeth. Then his voice hardened, "Cross me, though, and yer won't know what's hit yer. Then yer'll be posted to the worst, shitty destroyer in the fleet." He paused and then tried to bellow, although his voice was thin and reedy, "Stand to ... Attention! ... All right." He addressed the three-striper, "Wheel 'em into that hut over there for the time being." He glanced at his check-board, "Short-arm inspection at 1200."

"Short-arm inspection!" Bunts gasped at the mention of the usual check for VD when a sailor was posted to a new duty. "I didn't have friggin' time to get a sniff of the barmaid's apron, let alone cock me leg over!"

Next to him, his running-mate Sparks commented unfeelingly, "Hard cheese, why don't yer write to the padre about it?"

Bunts stuck his middle finger up and made a rude comment. His oppo was unperturbed. "Can't," he said easily, "Already got a No. 49 bus up there." And with that profound statement he and the rest started to drift over to the rusty Nissen hut. The three-striper smiled, but then he always smiled.

It was thus while they were engaged in the short arm inspection outside the Nissen hut that Guy de Gray spotted them as he went somewhat apprehensively toward the office of the Flag-Officer-in-Charge, Portsmouth. The draft was stood in three ranks, bell-bottoms round their naked ankles, shirts or vests rolled up about their waists. Walking slowly but purposefully down the files was a naval doctor, followed a pansy-looking orderly and the three-striper. At the latter's command, "Hold John Thomas!," the man to be inspected would grasp his penis and raise it so that the MO could see it clearly.

For his part, the latter, eyes gleaming behind his horn-rims, would inspect the organ as if it were of great importance, while the pansy-orderly, all malicious grins, waited with his pencil and pad to take the name of anyone caught with the dreaded 'social disease'.

As always, the young officer blushed at the sight, especially as the three-striper paused in the middle of his duties and threw up a great, smiling salute. Guy wished at that moment that the ground would open up and swallow him.

"Up, two, three!" the three-striper was intoning as a red-faced Guy de Gray returned the salute and hurried on, in the same moment that the matelot being inspected raised his garment and revealed his all to the surgeon-lieutenant, who began tut-tutting as if he had seen some social disease the like of which he had never come across before.

"Morning, Guy!" the Flag-Officer greeted him; he was a big, burly man in his late forties, lines of worry now etched on his once good-humoured face. Guy told himself that the Vice-Admiral looked as if he had a tough war so far. He indicated a chair and pushed a silver cigarette-case in the young sub's direction. "Smoke if you wish." He paused and shot Guy a searching look. Yet again, Guy flushed an embarrassed red.

"You won't remember me, Guy," he said. "You were just a kid when I sailed East, but I did serve with your father — God bless him — in the last show as a young sub, and I've known your mother for years since. Thought I'd like to marry her back in the 1920s, but their Lordships wouldn't have it. Too junior to warrant a marriage allowance — you know how it was in those days."

Guy de Gray didn't know, but he remained silent as if he understood.

"Well, Guy," the Admiral went on. "I had a call from your mother last night saying that you were coming here and asking me if I would keep an eye on you."

Inwardly, Guy groaned, his flush deepening even more. It was typical of his mother — 'marooned in Eastbourne' as she put it, all bloody cosy chats over weak tea with the neighbours and the weekly stint at the WVS. She was always so damned over-protective.

"I'll try my best, of course. I see that you've mucked about in boats a bit, which is useful. You can't beat seamanship, even in today's technological navy. Your course, I hear, was shorted. But you come from the finest naval stock. I think on account of that you'll cope come what may. What?"

Guy heard himself giving an enthusiastic response, though he had never felt less eager. He was always far too aware of his own failings. Still, he knew he must not let 'Mummy' and the family down.

"Now then, Guy, you must understand that I cannot give you exact details of your posting. Indeed, I should not be telling you this, but I know that you'll keep it under your hat and I feel I owe an obligation to your parents." He cleared his throat noisily and in spite of his broad, bluff face Guy de Gray had a suspicion that the Vice-Admiral was somewhat of an emotional man beneath his intimidating exterior.

"I can tell you this. You are to be posted to a great ship with a splendid tradition behind it. Unfortunately it has seen better days and the old-timers who have seen it through some very rough squalls are all gone. When she goes to sea again there'll be a nucleus of old-timers and regulars manning her, but most of the crew will be made up of Hostilities Only ratings and chaps from the Wavy Navy like yourself." He was referring to the part-time officers with their wavy stripes of the auxiliaries, which gave them their contemptuous name among the regulars.

"So you see, Guy," he continued, "it's going to be a tough, a very tough assignment indeed. You'll have to make decisions that in peacetime no one in his right mind would expect an officer of your age and experience to make." He shrugged. "But you'll do it, I know that. It's in the blood. All right, Lieutenant Gray, that's about it," the Vice-Admiral snapped formally.

Guy rose hastily to his feet, flushing as usual, and reached for his cap prior to saluting.

The Vice-Admiral gave him one last hard glance, as if seeing him for the last time, then as if he were back on the quarter-deck of the cruiser that had sunk beneath him off Crete earlier in the year, he barked, "All right, you'd better cut along — and good luck!"

De Gray saluted, but the senior officer seemed not to notice. It was as if the young, baby-faced sub-lieutenant had not been there at all.

Chapter Five

Dr Dietrich felt out of his depth. Back in his department at the University of Gottingen he had ruled the staff and students like a minor god. His *Assistenten* had jumped when he spoke. Graduate students wiped his blackboard clean for him before lectures. Students bowed and scraped whenever he made an appearance, all very much concerned to 'polish the visage', as they called it, in his presence so that he would favour them in their *vivas.* More than once, female students, even those who wore the brown uniform of leaders in the League of German Maidens, had made it quite clear that they were prepared to sleep with him if he looked favourably on them when examination time came round.

Here, however, at the headquarters of the Greater German General Staff in Berlin's Bendlerstrasse, his position was totally reversed. In spite of the fact that he was Goebbels' personal representative there, no one seemed to pay the slightest attention to him. Indeed, some of the more aristocratic army and navy officers actually appeared to be looking down their long noses disdainfully at him when he mentioned the Minister's name.

Besides, everything was so confusing, with staff officers striding purposefully back and forth as if they knew everything; telephones jingling, typewriters and teleprinters clattering incessantly. There were great rooms, guarded by wooden-faced, rigid, armed sentries, through the doors of which he glimpsed maps covering whole walls. In other rooms, field marshals hunched over sandpits while full generals moved their model soldiers and tanks about. Now and then he came across other rooms in which high-ranking officers gathered reverently, almost standing to attention as they listened to the red telephone through which the Fuehrer's own personal orders came. But nowhere in this great edifice in the centre of Berlin's government district could he seem to find out what the Greater German General Staff had planned for that damned Tommy aircraft carrier, the *Ark Royal.* That was, until he met the Commander of the U-Boat Weapon. Admiral Karl Doenitz. Then, after he had spoken to the lean officer with his killer's eyes set in a stern face, things started to happen.

Doenitz felt nothing but contempt for the ex-professor in his ill-fitting *Wehrmacht* uniform, with its sole decoration, the War Service Cross, Third Class, the one they gave to air-raid wardens and the like for 'outstanding service'. All the same, Karl Doenitz, out to make a name for himself before he was too old and pensioned off, realised the vital importance of having a key figure in Goebbels' propaganda *apparat* as an ally. He knew, too, that if his own submarine arm could sink the *Ark Royal,* something which the capital ships of his superior, Admiral Raeder, had been unable to do so far, it would be such a feather in his cap that he might well be Raeder's successor.

So over the next few days he put himself out for the ex-professor of English. There were two questions uppermost in his mind in connection with the *Ark Royal.* One, how long would it take to re-fit her and have her ready for sea-going duty, and, two, where would that sea-going duty take her?

He obtained the answer to the first question quite quickly and easily. The Prime Minister Churchill was only too eager to show the world that the *Ark Royal* would soon be ready for battle duty once more. And again the Press were invited into the shipyard to see the progress being made on repairs, not only the British Press but that of neutral foreign countries and the military attachés of those neutrals. Churchill knew that these attachés were a vital conduit for conveying military and naval information overseas and eventually into the hands of the enemy.

Churchill, that 'drunken sot of a British Prime Minister', knew that those uniformed neutrals could be bought by anyone, friend or foe, prepared to pay the asking price. Doenitz paid this price and obtained the information. "According to those paid foreign lackeys and amateur spies, Churchill is not having a proper re-fit done on *Ark Royal.* She is being patched up. Churchill needs the propaganda victory of having her afloat as soon as possible despite what certain people in the Ministry of Propaganda say." He looked pointedly at Dr Dietrich as if it were his fault. Dietrich ignored the look. He had seen through Doenitz by now. The hard-faced Admiral, who had been a U-boat skipper in World War One until the English had sunk his craft and captured him, was out for personal glory. "In addition," Doenitz continued, "the British are running short of carriers in Home Waters. Now with the *Amis* soon pouring troops across the Atlantic to the British Isles, Churchill needs every aircraft carrier available to guard the *Ami* convoys. So the *Ark Royal* is being made seaworthy. There is no time to do any more."

"So, *Herr Admiral?"* Dietrich jumped the gun, hoping that this was the information that Goebbels needed, enabling him to get out of this terrible and intimidating HQ where they had no respect for a German professor.

Doenitz frowned. "Your guess is as good as mine. I hope not, though."

"Why?"

But the Admiral did not answer that meaningful question, Instead, he swept through the great, sprawling HQ like a whirlpool and now Dietrich could see why his U-boat men admiringly called Doenitz *'der Grosse Lord'* — the Big Lord. He was indeed very masterful, brooking no opposition, sweeping all objections to one side as he took Dietrich to obscure little rooms on the top of the building, where lonely radio operators tapped into the weather from the Arctic Circle to the Azores; into heavily guarded rooms where every single curtained map had its personal guard of an NCO and two ratings, then right down to the cellars where most of the staff seemed to be foreigners and where he could pick out at least six European languages.

Finally, after an exhausting afternoon, while a weary professor sipped weak China tea, and a seemingly fresh Doenitz twice his age downed his favourite North German schnapps — '*Schlichte'* — the latter attempted to sum up his findings of that long day.

Pointing at the map of Europe adorning one wall of the little office, the only sound as the afternoon darkened being the soft tread of the naval sentry outside in the corridor, Doenitz fingered his glass thoughtfully and started to explain. "One of the problems of sinking an aircraft carrier is the aircraft they carry, *Herr Professor.* You see, these ships are mostly lightly armoured, though the flight-deck of the *Ark Royal* is constructed of steel, unlike those of the American carriers. Their aircraft can keep any attacker at considerable range until help can be summoned to ward off surface attackers. You understand?" He looked at a weary Dietrich the way the professor himself would have looked when some stupid student had been unable to grasp the principles of the use of the apostrophe.

"Yes."

Doenitz continued, "So that is why I said I hope Churchill wouldn't employ the *Ark Royal* in the North Atlantic. Too much space out there and too many capital ships from the British Home Fleet to call on." He downed his fiery, colourless schnapps, rose to his feet and crossed to the map. With a sweep of his skinny, almost claw-like hand, he encompassed first Norway and then the Central Mediterranean. "These German-occupied territories are both vital to the Reich's war effort. At the moment, as you well know, *Herr Professor,* all is quiet in Norway since last spring's fighting. Down there in the Mediterranean things are different. Due to the well-known cowardice of our allies, the Italian spaghetti-eaters, we are involved in their war against the Tommies in North Africa."

He turned from the map and faced Dietrich. Like a schoolmaster staring at a rather backward pupil he asked, "If you were that Jewish lackey Churchill, to which theatre of war do you think you'd send the *Ark Royal?"* He looked impatiently at the ex-professor, as if he had been rarely faced by such an idiotic pupil.

Dietrich felt himself colouring as his brain raced wildly, trying to find a satisfactory answer to the Admiral's question. Finally, he stuttered hesitantly, "I suppose because the *Ark Royal* is not completely repaired, or won't be when she next goes to sea, he'd pick Norway, where nothing is going on at the moment. Is that what you want to know, *Herr Admiral?"*

Doenitz did not react. Instead, he answered the question with one of his own. "What would be the advantage — to us — if Churchill did?" He answered his own question, obviously rhetorical. "The *Ark Royal* would be confined to Norway's narrow fiords where the ship herself would be vulnerable from the land. More than that, all the land area is under German control and dominated by our aircraft. I don't think it would take too long for our Fifth Air Fleet up there to deal with the semi-obsolete biplanes that fly from the *Ark Royal.* Then the carrier would be at the mercy of my U-boats. They would make short work of her, unprotected as she would be by surface ships and her own planes."

Dietrich seemed to look a little brighter. It seemed that the schoolmaster/schoolboy relationship between Doenitz and himself was over. "So that's that, eh, *Herr Admiral?* I can report to the Minister that once the Tommy ship is in Norwegian waters she's — er — a dead duck, as you would say." He smiled.

Doenitz looked down with contempt at the man's broad, complacent, civilian's face. "Like a dead duck? I don't think so, *Herr Professor.* No one, as yet, has predicted that Churchill has planned to send her to the North. There is nothing going on there at the moment that calls for the presence of the *Ark Royal."*

Dietrich looked crestfallen. "What do I tell the Minister, then?" he asked plaintively, knowing that he was completely out of his depth with these military people.

Doenitz leaned forward, his lean, hard face reflecting his bitter inner tension, as if he hated wasting time like this when he could be tackling the enemy — and beating him. "Tell him this. Your Minister can drop a word in the Fuehrer's ear to give me complete freedom of action in the Mediterranean."

"Mediterranean?"

Doenitz did not seem to hear. "If we can get the *Ark Royal* into that enclosed sea, with both shores lined by countries under our control, the ship doesn't stand a chance." He paused, breathing a little hard as if he had just carried out some strenuous exercise. "Once the Tommy carrier passes the safety of Gibraltar and our people start plotting her position for the attack, she's finished. She'll never pass Gibraltar and out of the Med again, *Herr Professor."*

Herr Professor der Anglistik Dr Dietrich was not an imaginative man, rather the opposite. But for a moment he quailed under that piercing look from the Admiral's blue eyes; he recognised the look of death.

Chapter Six

Pay night in Pompey.

Two hours before, the draft had been lined up in their Nissen hut, washed and shaved, pay-books at the ready, caps set at the approved regulation angle.

Opposite them at the trestle table, covered by a rough Navy blanket, sat young Sub-Lieutenant de Gray, and next to him, hunched over the money, sat a pudgy pay-master petty officer named Callaghan, wearing glasses and looking like a careful hedgehog.

Under the gimlet eye of CPO Drake, the ratings of the draft had advanced one by one to receive their pay, less 'stoppages' for lost or stolen forks, toothbrushes and the like. As Callaghan called out the name, the rating stepped forward and CPO Drake had barked, "Officer on parade — *salute!* Cap off to receive pay."

Like automata they had done so, signed for their meagre pay and strained to hear Callaghan say, "Don't waste your money, laddie. Keep away from the pleasures of the flesh." He would then beam owl-like through his thick glasses and add: "Nice baked beans on toast at the Sally Ann and six-penn'orth at the pictures and you'll be well away. Next!" Then CPO Drake had taken over again with a sharp "About turn ... quick march ... let's be havin' yer, me lucky lads!"

That had been just before tea. Now it was dark, with Portsmouth carefully blacked out, no lights visible save those of the searchlights, parting the dark night sky with icy fingers in search of the German intruders who came over the great naval base every night. But if all was blacked out, there was plenty of hectic life behind the shutters of the many pubs lining the Hard and frequented by sailors. The whores, amateur and professional, were busy too as they always were on pay-nights; in the doorways of the bombed ruins, flashing their torches on and off to attract customers, adding their usual terms of cheap endearment and offers. "Fancy a nice time, duckie ... Give yer yer money's worth ... As clean as a Somerset virgin ... yer won't get no nasty disease off'n me, sailorboy!"

"Why clean as a Somerset virgin?" the Irishman Sparks asked idly and without too much interest as he kicked a beer can down the gutter, littered with crumpled pieces of greasy fish-and-chip wrapping paper.

They had shared a gill of beer in one of the Hard's poorer pubs, where they still scattered sawdust on the floor and spittoons were placed at strategic places, and discussed the problem which was uppermost in their minds — women.

"Holy Mother of Jesus!" Sparks had exclaimed, taking his turn to sup at the glass of beer, watched by a careful Bunts. "It's so long since I had it, I don't know where to put it no more!"

"Yer get yer share," his running-mate commented, "and watch where you're puttin' all that ale. Yer not getting much more than a crafty wank for a quid and that's all each of us has got."

"No crafty wanks," Sparks had said firmly, handing the glass to the big Yorkshireman. "Every night I slip into me pit with a problem on me mind and each morning I wake up with the solution in me hand. No, none of that stuff — I want the real thing, matey!"

"Well, yer not gonna get it on the kind of money you've got. Them Judies'll want thirty bob at least before they spread their pearly gates and even then they'll be friggin' moaning that they might as well be a friggin' charity." The two mates lapsed into a gloomy silence.

For a few minutes they watched the activities at the dingy bar, lit by a flickering, evil-smelling petroleum lantern. There, a drunken civvie with the brick-red face of an alcoholic was swallowing razor-blades for a bet, while next to him an equally drunken matelot was warbling unsteadily: *"I've got sixpence, jolly, jolly sixpence. I've got sixpence to last me all me life. I've got tuppence to spend, tuppence to lend and tuppence to send home to the wife. No cares have I to grieve me ..."*

"Put a friggin' sock in it!" someone yelled in a disgruntled voice, while the drunken civvie said, "I'm gonna take me teeth out now, gents, so you can see my cuts when I swallow this 'ere Gillette blade."

Suddenly, Bunts forgot the matelot and the drunk. He pressed the big Irishman's arm and said, "Listen, you big Mick, I think I can see a way for both of us to dip our wicks on the money we've got."

Sparks looked at his running-mate as if he had gone mad. "Has that gnat's piss gone to yer friggin' head or summat? Its only half a gill yer know and I allus thought you was a ten-pint a night man!"

"I am. But I'm not talking about beer now. I'm talking beaver — B-E-A-V-E-R. Now this is what I suggest, so pin back yer lug-holes and listen ..."

Sub-Lieutenant Guy de Gray couldn't sleep. The little cabin at the far end of the Nissen hut was too close to the heads, naval latrines, and his nostrils were constantly assailed by the stink of Jeyes' Fluid and stale urine. Also, although it was past Lights Out, he could still hear groans and muted sighs from the big room outside his and he didn't need a crystal ball to tell him what was causing them. He remembered the same sort of thing from his years at boarding school before he volunteered for the Royal Navy.

He sighed and wondered if things would have been different if he had been brought up by his father rather than by his genteel, over-protective mother, with her ladies sewing circle, high teas complete with cake stand and fine bone china, and all her attempts to keep up appearances on a small naval pension.

It certainly hadn't been the right training for the rough-and-tumble of lower-deck naval life. The boys he commanded were years older in the wisdom of the streets than he ever would be. They'd half-inched, as they called it openly, from Woolies, they'd written rude words on the walls, and they'd even touched-up girls in the back alleys of their industrial home towns. In the darkness of his bunk with its rough blankets he blushed at the very thought. He'd never 'touch-up' a girl, he thought miserably, even if he lived to be a hundred, which he somehow suspected he wouldn't.

He swallowed hard and gingerly touched his genitals. His penis was beginning to stiffen and he cursed and remembered his mother's warnings when he was about to go to boarding school as a thirteen-year-old, veiled hints which he had barely understood about 'self-pollution' and 'thinking naughty thoughts', whatever they were. He abruptly withdrew his hand from between his legs.

Guy closed his eyes firmly and tried to forget that other thing. Instead, he concentrated on promising himself that he would be a good officer and do his best for these rough young men whom he would soon be taking to sea. He dare not fail, for their lives may be at stake. He would soon have to live up to what his dead father, the man who he had never seen, would have expected from him. *He just had to do the right thing!*

Outside, as he drifted into an uneasy sleep, the sirens started give their thin wails and over at Gosport the heavy ack-ack began to thud away. It didn't wake him, like most boys of his time and generation he had become accustomed to hearing gunfire.

He dreamed he was back in the overly-decorated seaside flat in Eastbourne, the piano laden with silver — framed, yellowing photographs of long-dead relations. They were polished before his mother's once-a-week morning bath — "Only nine inches of water, dear, just like dear Mr Churchill has." Even when the cleaning lady came on Wednesdays his mother never allowed her to touch those precious photographs, they were her life.

His mother was taking tea with the ladies circle, being gracious and charming as she poured weak tea out (the charwoman used to call it 'consumptive muck') from the treasured Queen Anne silver teapot. Suddenly there was a shrill scream. The idle chatter of the ladies in their floral dresses stopped. The ceiling crumbled and plaster dust floated down, followed by snapped lathes. There was the acrid, pungent smell of spent explosive. Cups overturned, plates tumbled to the floor and shattered.

Then as suddenly as it had started, the noise ceased. It was replaced by a steady dripping sound. Hovering in Guy's dream in the far corner of the shattered ceiling, looking down at the shambles below, young Guy de Gray was shocked.

The liquid from the overturned cups, which dripped on to the lace tablecloth and from there to the fine Persian rug — his mother's pride — was not pale, weak tea, but *blood!*

"The rotten buggers, to jew me like that!" the middle-aged whore cursed, her knickers still heaped round her ankles; either she had forgotten to pull them up as the shore patrol approached, or perhaps it didn't matter. "They ain't got no heart, doing that to a poor old working hoor like me!" She dabbed at her raddled cheeks and the handkerchief came away brick-red with cheap rouge. "I hope they fucking sink next time those sods go to sea!"

Standing in the gloomy pub corridor under the faded sign reading "NO CHILDREN UNDER THE AGE OF 18", CPO Drake eyed the prostitute, together with the men of the shore patrol who had been summoned by her cries for help. They did not know whether to laugh at her with her faded knickers and veiled hat tilted crazily on her hennaed head, or take pity on her for being 'jewed', as she called it, out of her rightful fee.

"What happened?" Drake asked finally, breaking into the racket she was making.

"What friggin' happened? I'll friggin' well tell yer, Chiefie. The one with the red hair was jumping up and down on top of me, pumping away as if he was tryin' to blow up a barrage balloon, when all of a sudden he went limp on me. I said to meself, 'He's done. I'll have time to nip round to the fish-shop just off the Hard and get mesen some grub.' I do love me fish and taties, out of the newspaper, with vinegar and — "

"Get on with it!" Drake snapped. "We ain't got all day!"

She muttered something obscene which the old CPO didn't quite catch, though he thought it wouldn't be wise to ask her to repeat it, and she continued, "But no, he hadn't come, he sez, and could he pop back down the lane for a quick pee. He said for me to look after the money and he'd take his change when he'd finished."

CPO Drake shook his grizzled head. The world was going mad, he thought. He restrained himself with difficulty and asked, "Well, what happened next?"

The whore shrugged her shoulders. "Well, he was back in a few shakes of a lamb's tail, fresh as a friggin' fighting cock and got going again as if he hadn't had it since the day war broke out, going at it like a fiddler's elbow, while I kept hold of his money. Then it struck me —"

"What?" Drake asked, his curiosity alive and kicking.

She glared at Drake. "It wasn't the same bloke. Not only did he not have red hair, but he spoke like some great Yorkshire lummox, and he had quite a different weapon altogether!"

Next to the CPO, a young sailor muttered incredulously, "Christ, she can tell the difference between tools in the dark!"

"I heard that!" the whore shrilled. "If you'd had as many as I have up you, rattling yer poor old bones, you'd be able to tell the difference, matey!"

"Sorry, miss!" said the young sailor hurriedly, scared that the enraged harridan would launch herself at him any second.

"So what you're saying," CPO Drake said carefully, "is that these two unknown sailors" — and the CPO was beginning to think that he already knew just who they were — "did it to you for the price of one?"

"Yer," the woman snapped, "the friggin' cheap-skates!"

"And what exactly do you want us to do, missus?"

"It's friggin' obvious, ain't it!" she snorted, "Find those men and get me outstanding money off 'em."

"There's thousands of matelots in Pompey," CPO Drake suggested carefully. "And there's a war on, yer know, missus."

"Frig the war! Nothing to do with me. I didn't friggin' well start it, did I!" She added accusingly, "And if you can't find them rotten swines, you can get on the blower to Mister Winston Churchill" — she pronounced the Prime Minister's name contemptuously — "he's got plenty of money, look at them big cigars he's allus smoking. Yer average worker couldn't afford them." Her raddled face contorted bitterly at the thought of the great injustice done to her while she served her country — on her back.

"I've done my bit, looking after the boys in blue, them friggin' Jack Tars. Let Churchill cough up. That's me final word!" she said, spitting in the road and pulling a crumpled Woodbine packet out of the leg of her knickers and lighting a cigarette with a defiant gesture.

"Phew!" the young sailor next to Drake whispered, "That's a turn up for the book, Chiefie. Writing to Winnie to cough up for a knee-trembler in a Pompey back-street!"

CPO Drake nodded his silent agreement. What was he going to do with this irate tart? But fortunately he was spared making a major decision, for at that moment a Naval 15 cwt truck came slowly down the Hard, stopping opposite Drake and his little group, with its loudspeaker blaring a recall.

"Is that you, Duggie?" a well-remembered voice called. It was Charlie Higgins, who had served on the China Station with him as an Able Seaman back in the 1920s.

"Yes. Where's the fire, Charlie?"

The middle-aged chief petty officer, with a well-rounded, comfortable stomach that indicated he was in good standing with the cooks in the galley, moved across to where Drake stood opposite the angry whore. The CPO took in the situation at a glance, he had seen such incidents often enough in his quarter of a century or so in the Royal Navy. "Solved the problem for you, Duggie," Higgins said heartily. "Everyone and his son are being recalled to barracks. There's a big flap on."

"What kind of flap, Charlie? The Jerries ain't landed on the South Coast or somewhere, have they?"

"No, nothing like that," Charlie laughed scornfully. He bent close to Drake's ear so that the others would not hear. "Got it from one of the ships' writers who should know — them jammy buggers know everything. He sez that it's in the Med. Something's going on in the Med. They're gonna have to ship out drafts in double-quick time. All right, get 'em moving!"

The shore patrol turned about smartly under Drake's orders, while the little blue-painted Navy van slowly went on its way, Higgins shouting the re-call through the loudspeaker on the roof.

"And wot about me, eh?" the angry whore called after the shore patrol.

CPO Duggie Drake had what he thought was a brilliant, witty answer for the irate woman. "Why don't you write to Mr Churchill, luv?" he shouted back. "He'll be all right for a couple of bob, I don't doubt!” And with that witty sally CPO Drake and his patrol vanished into the Pompey darkness, heading for the unknown.

Chapter Seven

The Stuka Ju 87 dive-bomber seemed to hover in the shimmering blue sky like a metallic hawk selecting its prey far down below on the island of Malta set in a glittering sea. Behind the Stuka, stacked up in what the harassed, sweating ack-ack gunners below called a 'cab-rank', other aircraft did the same. To port and starboard, the eager Me 109 fighters, with the evil, crooked cross on their tails, and the more vulnerable Italian G.50 Freccia Fiat fighters, zipped back and forth across the heavens waiting for any fighter from Malta to rise and take up the unequal challenge. So far, however, everything on the embattled Mediterranean island below remained in tense, expectant silence. The defences, hard pressed as they were, were not going to waste precious ammunition and the pitifully few planes until they knew from which direction the main attack would come.

The Stuka leader had seen his target for this sortie, and he sighed wearily. He was sick of that damned British island and seemed to have spent a lifetime bombing it. But they were still there, those precious oil tanks, badly camouflaged (there was no decent netting left on the island to hide them). It would be so easy to knock them out. Once the oil, the life-blood of the island, had gone the few remaining, battered aircraft which defended it would be useless and the place was finished, ripe for plucking by the German *Falschirmerjager* and Italian airborne troops. They were already waiting in Greece and Sicily, ready to launch their aerial assault.

The Stuka leader waggled his distinctive, inverted gull-shaped wings; the signal to attack. He lowered his dive-brakes and automatic dive-control, then the aircraft hurtled down out of the blue and the raid was on! With its siren, mounted on the streamlined, fixed landing gear, going full blast and giving a banshee wail, the pilot headed for the ground at over 300 mph. Behind him, plane after plane peeled off and plummeted down after him.

Now the flak opened up, with brown and grey puff-balls from the exploding shells peppering the sky. The diving Stukas were rocked from side to side as shell-blasts exploded near them. They seemed to bear a charmed life, emerging from the smoke of very near shell bursts and continuing their head-long attack.

The wing leader felt himself beginning to black out as the G-force pushed him hard against his back-rest. His face was flattened and distorted and, starved of their blood supply, a black veil began to slip down over his eyes. It was now or never. He pressed the bomb toggle and relieved of its load the Stuka shuddered and lurched as the 500 lb bomb left its belly.

As the bomb screeched down towards its target the Stuka slowly pulled out of the dive, every rivet protesting. The ground rose to meet him and for a moment the pilot thought he was not going to make it and he was about to smash into the stony ground. Then the controls responded, the nose began to lift and the dive-bomber soared back up into the sky. The pilot slumped in his seat, gasping and lathered in sweat, while plane after plane copied his attack of death and destruction.

Five minutes later the medium bombers made their run. They had come in two squadrons from their bases in Sicily, 60 miles away. Now they spread out in pairs and flew in at about 280 mph over St Paul's Bay, near the northern tip of battered Malta.

All the time the ack-ack guns barked at them, their shells slamming into the sky in crazy profusion. But round and round flew the He 111s, seeming to crawl like evil black spiders through the smoke-peppered blue sky. Five minutes later the Heinkels reformed over the sea. Now that the ack-ack fire had ceased, a now-obsolete biplane Gloster Sea Gladiator — one of only four on the island — was sent up to intercept them, but it lasted only a matter of moments. A Fiat Freccia screeched across the island at roof-top level, leaving lines of washing fluttering madly, then its two 0.5 in. machine-guns began chattering.

The British aircraft was no match for the Freccia and the Italian showed no mercy as his rounds poured into the Gladiator and metal splinters flew off the wings and fuselage. Frantically, the RAF pilot tried to keep airborne, then he was hit and slumped over the shattered controls, dying as his plane went into its last dive.

The German bombers came in again, with nothing to stop them. They flew in in three nose-to-tail lines and the ack-ack took up the challenge once more. The leading He 111 was hit and a jet of white smoke poured from its port engine, turning immediately to thick black smoke, and the plane swerved violently to starboard, slamming into the nearest aircraft in the tight formation. There was a flash and a second later another huge explosion of blinding light. Bits and pieces of metal fuselage mixed with engine parts, under-carriages, and human debris rained down.

The battle for Malta was reaching a crisis. Down below at his HQ, General Lord Gort, VC the Governor, with his tough, hard-bitten soldier's face, reached a decision. "Radio links?" he asked the anxious-looking naval and air force commanders, watching the desperate aerial battle with him.

"Incredibly distorted. Lots of static, Jerry traffic, enemy brass bands blaring full out to create interference," the naval commander answered, not taking his eyes off the battle that could be seen through the shattered window.

"Courier seaplane to Alexandria?" Gort persisted grimly. He had once led the defeated British Expeditionary Force from the beaches at Dunkirk. That defeat had meant the end of his Army career. Now, it seemed he was predestined to preside over another great defeat: the loss of Britain's most vital possession in the Central Mediterranean.

"On fire in the harbour off Valetta," the air force representative answered, "And —" he suddenly groaned. "Christ Almighty, are we not to be spared anything, Lord Gort?"

"What is it?"

"The Huns have downed another of our Gladiators," the Group Captain answered, his voice sinking. "There are only two left. Great balls of fire — what *are* we going to do?"

As if by way of the answer, mocking the pathetic attempts by the British to save the embattled island, a Heinkel came in low, its monstrous shadow being dragged behind it over the sun-baked ruins, its machine-guns blazing away at the forward HQ. Stone walls and window glass splintered, spent bullets ricocheted to left and right, dry-as-dust timbers began to blaze.

Gort knew it was time for decision, however risky. The authorities back in London had to know — absolutely clearly — just how precarious was the situation in Malta. The island urgently needed aviation fuel and aircraft for defence and attack if it was going to survive as a base to aid the great push in North Africa against the German Afrika Korps. If those supplies did not get through and Malta was lost, the 1941 attack in Africa would fail because the Germans and their Italian allies would have total command of this part of the Mediterranean. Their ships would be able to cross the *Mare Nostrum,* as the Italian dictator Benito Mussolini had proudly declared the Med, with impunity. The enemy would be able to supply their North African front how, where and when they liked. They would have nothing to fear from the British in the Mediterranean.

"Defiant!" yelled Gort above the racket as another stick of bombs screamed down, exploding and making the building shudder.

"The *Defiant* will have to run the gauntlet with a personal message from me to the PM!" He said this without waiting for their protests, knowing that already new enemy forces were being readied in Sicily to continue the attack by night. Then it would be impossible to leave the hard-pressed island, for by then the Italian submarines would be on the prowl offshore, the fires caused by the bombing silhouetting anything leaving the harbour.

Hastily, Gort started to write out a message in long-hand, knowing that there would not be time to encode it. Anyway, it didn't matter — if the little torpedo-boat got through. If she didn't, encoded or not, the message would go to the bottom of the Med with *Defiant.*

Half-an-hour later, the young skipper of the lithe, fast *Defiant,* dark weariness circles under his eyes, made his last inspection of the boat. Her superstructure had already been well lashed by shrapnel from the German bombs. There were huge gaps and tears everywhere and splinters of wood lay on the littered deck.

Her radio mast hung precariously by its support wires, the loose aerial spitting dangerous blue sparks as it swung and touched metal, while the radio operator tried desperately to get the set working before they left harbour at dusk. Fortunately there had been no serious casualties among the crew except for one or two pale-faced matelots who had been nicked by flying debris and were now bandaged and able to carry out their duties until they reached the Forces General Hospital in Gibraltar.

There was, however, one great problem. A bomb had breached the dock, which was flooding rapidly. The water level had risen over 20 ft, but that was not the real danger, for an ammunition lighter, still partly filled with HE, was in a dry dock only yards away from the plucky *Defiant.* If the water level reached the lighter's hull she would be swept helplessly into the dock, blocking *Defiant's* passage to sea. Out of control, she could ram the motor-torpedo-boat and that, the hard-pressed skipper in his tarnished white cap told himself, would be that. He prayed as he set off to report to Dock HQ that the pumps for the dry-dock, which were already working flat out, would keep the water level down and the ammunition lighter in position until the *Defiant* had sailed. Then it would be Devil take the hindmost.

But the *Defiant* was not yet on her way with the vital appeal from Lord Gort and it seemed as if the enemy sensed the importance of her role, for as the hard-working Maltese peasants and dock workers settled down for their last meal of the day — fires were not allowed after dark as part of the air-raid precautions — another flight of Focke-Wulf 190 fighter-bombers came winging their way in, straight for Valetta. They came in at sea level with the setting sun behind them, blinding the anti-aircraft gunners at their weapons ringing the Grand Harbour.

Half-blinded, but alerted by the roar and snarl of nine fast planes at full throttle, the gunners fired round after round at them. But the *Luftwaffe* pilots were experienced and came in weaving from side to side in line ahead, sometimes so low they were obscured by the waves — and this time the enemy were using torpedoes. Immediately they were in range the German planes dropped their torpedoes. While the crew of *Defiant,* those who had no weapons, could only hold their breath and pray.

As the last of the enemy planes winged their way across the darkening Mediterranean, leaving behind them yet more death and destruction, with great mushrooms of smoke rising into the sky over the battered island, Gort made his decision. He approached the young skipper, a look of near-pleading on his rough-hewn face. Gort no longer looked like the man who had won his VC for bravery in the trenches in the Old War and had commanded the BEF a war later; instead there was something old and defeated about his features.

"You've got to get through, Lieutenant Baldwick," he stated. "We're running out of ammo, oil, planes. There's just enough food left for a month — at half-rations — for the civvies and our men. We're fast coming to the end of the road!"

'Baldy', as he was known to his mess-mates, although he had a fine head of hair, looked embarrassed. It was disconcerting for the twenty-year-old to be addressed like this by a Field Marshal, who was almost three times his age.

"Yessir," he answered. "The *Defiant* will do it, sir!"

"Good show, Baldwick," Gort said, like a man clutching at a straw. "With luck, if you sail within the next half-hour — and you must because we're running out of fuel for the pumps which are trying to keep the ammo lighter in the dry-dock — with God's help you should reach Gibraltar by dawn tomorrow. Then this message must go off to the PM at once. You understand, without a moment's delay — *AT ONCE!*

The young naval officer was impressed. As his cronies would have said: "You're pissing with the big dogs now, old chap!" He managed to stutter, "You can rely on me, sir, my chaps and the *Defiant.* We'll get through if anyone can."

Gort seemed to be cheered by the young man's enthusiasm and confidence. He clapped his hand on the officer's hard shoulder, wishing that he was young, bold and confident again, saying, "I'm sure you will. And remember, there'll be a gong in it for you if you make it."

"Thank you, sir. I — we — are not doing it for any gongs, sir, but for the sake of the old country and the King-Emperor." He flushed a faint pink at his unaccustomed rhetoric.

"Well said, Baldwick, well said!" Gort gave a faint sigh, perhaps even one of relief as he realised that now the burden had been taken off his shoulders. He could do no more.

As the light went, *Defiant* was on her way 25 minutes later, edging her progress through the wrecks in the harbour, every man aboard her knowing that if they failed Malta would be swallowed up by the enemy and Africa would be lost.

Part Two

The Voyage Out

Chapter One

"Cor, ferk a duck!" one of the new draft cried out in wonder as he looked up at the great flight-deck of the *Ark Royal* towering high above the sailors halted on the wet quayside below. "What a whopper!"

"She's 25,000 tons water displacement," someone informed the matelots, laden down with their sea-going gear. "Biggest carrier in the Royal Navy!"

CPO Drake, still stiff from his bunk in the Nissen hut, had thought it better not to go home for the night; it would only have caused Maggie to weep. So he had telephoned her at the corner-shop grocer's and, using the old private code, he had told his wife, "I'm off ... Yer can guess where." She had sobbed, but that had been all.

Drake gazed up at the *Ark,* as he called her. She had been patched up well, considering the time the dockies and dock-yard tiffies had spent aboard. But the riveting was rough and ready and not properly finished and although the buckled plates had been cleaned and straightened before being riveted back in their places, here and there he could still see the burn-marks and the odd depression. If the *Ark* was heading for the Med, as he thought she was, the skipper would have to be careful in the Bay of Biscay. That notoriously wild stretch of water would soon rip the damaged plates off her before she ever reached the Med.

Standing a little way apart from the curious draft, Guy de Gray was both interested and apprehensive. The Vice-Admiral had been right, thought Guy, he had been posted to a great ship with a splendid fighting tradition, but that in itself worried him. Could he live up to that tradition? He flushed at the thought that he might not be capable enough. It was almost as if his long-dead father was glancing over his shoulder, watching him carefully, checking how he was going to react to this new challenge. He made a conscious effort and said to himself, "I shall do my best, Dad ... I won't let you down, I promise."

"You talking to yourself, Lieutenant?" a hard, yet pleasant voice snapped.

Guy turned, startled. A lieutenant-commander in his late twenties stood there. His uniform was old and faded and his cap was equally battered, with the gold braid long tarnished and green with verdigris. But on the breast of his tunic he wore the ribbons of the DSC and DSO, a high decoration for such a comparatively young officer. At that moment, Guy envied him more than anyone else. Fancy having two gongs like that before you were thirty!

"No, sir ... I wasn't, sir," he stuttered, going even more red-faced. He saluted almost as an after-thought.

The lieutenant-commander returned the salute casually, as if it was not very important, and said, "Well, if you don't talk to yourself now, you will be doing so once you've finished your first spell in the old *Ark.* We certainly seem to attract trouble from old Jerry!" He laughed and added, "You must be Gray?"

"Yessir," Guy replied promptly.

"Good show. Welcome aboard the *Ark.*" He turned to an attentive CPO Drake, who was making his own assessment of the carelessly-attired officer, who seemed to be vaguely familiar to the old CPO. "Get the draft aboard, Chiefie ... Chiefie Drake, yes, that's it!"

Drake looked puzzled.

"You don't remember me, do you?" the lieutenant-commander said. "I'm Carter. You told me off many a time when I was a young snotty in the *Warspite* before the war. Remember?"

"Yessir, I remember now, sir. You was the one who brought that donkey aboard for the foreign admiral's party —"

"Eh ... well ..." Carter hurriedly interrupted the CPO. "Don't want your young officers to form a bad opinion of me already, do we! Bolshie as I was in those days, Mr Gray's going to find out just what sort of swine I am soon enough. All right, wheel 'em aboard, Chiefie."

"Aye, aye, sir," Drake answered smartly. Gray could see that it was obvious the CPO liked the lieutenant-commander. More his type, probably, and added a little miserably to himself — "Not like me, naturally."

"Now then, Gray," the officer said as Drake started to march his men up the companion-way to the lower-deck, which seemed miles above them, "let's tackle our problem first."

"Problem, sir?"

"Yes." He opened a silver cigarette-case and offered it to Gray. "Have a gasper, old chap." Gray didn't smoke but he thought it wiser to accept a 'Capstan'. He allowed the lieutenant-commander to light it for him, coughing and spluttering as badly as he had done when he had tried his first cigarette back in prep-school in what seemed another age.

"Watch that cough of your, Gray!" the officer commented and dismissed the matter immediately. "Now I know that you and your chaps are trained for ordinary sea duties. With the exception of your 'Sparks' and 'Bunts' you have no specialists in the draft. Well, I'm afraid, for better or worse, you're going to be immediate specialists."

"How do you mean, sir?"

"Gunners, that's what you are going to become. We lost our last lot of Tail-end Charlies on our way back, poor devils. Those are the chaps who manned the banks of machine-guns aft of the bridge — 'Chicago pianos' the matelots call them. Now we need all the trained gunners we can get. The already-trained men in other drafts are going elsewhere in this ship. So you are the new Tail-end Charlies, I'm afraid. They're easier to learn how to handle and you'll have to work up your chaps on the voyage out."

"To where, sir?" Gray just had to ask.

Lieutenant-Commander Carter shook his head. "I'm still under sealed orders. I'm afraid. Won't know our destination until the skipper breaks the seal, probably tomorrow when we're well out to sea. So once you're settled in, Gray, get cracking. CPO Drake'll help you, he's a good man. They say he's been at sea since the days of Nelson and the wooden walls. Wouldn't surprise me if he didn't fight at Trafalgar, he's that old."

With that, Carter bustled away to meet another batch of the new draft to give them their orders, leaving de Gray slightly perturbed and wondering what a Chicago piano looked like, because the last time he had fired any weapon it had been a hand-gun on the range in his first year of training.

"All right, as long as you shower of muvvers' darlings play ball with me, I'll play ball with you," CPO Drake was saying gruffly as the draft assembled in their mess, over-crowded and already lumbered with their gear as was customary in wartime ships. "You an' me will get on together like a house on fire." His somewhat harsh tone diminished as he realised once again just how young and lost most of the new matelots seemed to be. He'd wager that not one of them had been to sea before.

He continued: "I am supposed to read you the Articles of War, lads, it is according to King's Regulations before you come aboard, with the exception of the Oxford men among you," he grinned, but his grin was not returned. These men were too serious. It was as if they had realised for the first time that they were actually going to war. "I don't suppose you'd have understood them, so I'll say this instead — just keep your noses clean and you'll be OK. This ship's yer home from now on, so keep it ship-shape and Bristol fashion. We're in for a lot of hard, new work — and perhaps a bit of danger as well. But then that's what the Navy is paying you all that money for!" That quip brought a few horse-laughs, but in general they were still subdued.

"I was blowed up a couple of times in the last show and I've been in the water off Crete for twelve hours in this lot. So you can expect a packet of trouble somewhere along the line. That goes without saying. So work hard, keep yer nose clean, listen carefully to what yer superiors say — and trust yer ship."

"Anything else, Chiefie?" cheekily asked the red-headed Mick, who Drake knew had been trained as a radio operator.

"Watch yer lip, Sparks," CPO Drake snapped, "I've already got me eye on you!"

Next to Mick, Bunts whispered, "I tell yer, it's that friggin' Judy from the other night, the cowbag gave me crabs as well!" He scratched his crotch gingerly.

"One last thing," Drake continued in his briefing, "I don't want a lot of green fruit, wet behind the ears still, to make a lash-up of things, so I'm gonna tell you this buckshee and for free, the only free thing you're likely to get in the Royal this side of Christmas. Most of the regulars on the *Ark* are locals, reservists who used to be fisherman in civvy street and yer average fisherman is a superstitious so-and-so. So you'll have to play the funny old game that they play — and don't ask me why they play it 'cos I'm not Jesus and don't know all the answers."

Someone muttered *sotto voce* that he thought that CPOs out-ranked God. Drake ignored the remark and said: "There's certain words you can't mention with fishermen 'cos they think it's bad luck — they're 'pig', 'fox', 'rabbit' or the like."

Sparks whistled softly through his teeth and said: "And I thought it was only yer old Irish biddy who was superstitious!"

Drake went on, "Nor do I want to see any of you matelots putting a hatch-cover on upside down, or anyone laying a ship's broom across a hawser, d'yer hear?"

"Why, Chiefie?" Bunts asked.

" 'Cos, yer great Yorkshire pudding, it's bad luck!" and Drake lowered his voice melodramatically, "More than likely the whole ship'll disappear if you get it wrong."

"Holy Mary, Mother of Jesus!" Sparks exclaimed, crossing himself.

"Take more than that to stop the jinx," Drake said. "That's what happened in one of our corvettes back in December 1940 when one of the hands smuggled in a couple of rabbits he'd been given by some tart just for the Christmas dinner. The corvette disappeared lock, stock and barrel. They never found a trace of her. Rabbits, yer see."

The draft were so impressed that they didn't even hear the approach of the heavy-footed Master-at-Arms, the dreaded ship's policeman, who came into the mess and, winking at Drake, said: "You tell 'em, Duggie!" He chuckled throatily and added: "And what happens to nancy boys who cross their good old Master-at-Arms?"

With a sigh, Drake gave up. Trust a Master-at-Arms to spoil everything, they always did. "All right!" he snapped, "Stow yer gear. I'll be around to have a look-see in an hour's time." Outside the mess, he turned to the beetle-browed Master-at-Arms, "Why do you allus spoil my stories, Alf?" he demanded, "I would have had 'em pissing down their right trouser-leg in half a mo." But he made the remark without conviction.

Two hours later de Gray had just finished making himself at home in the tiny steel box called his cabin, arranging the silver-framed photograph of his mother in her silk gown, patting her pet Peke and looking very matronly. Next to it went a picture of his father, in uniform complete with stiff collar and looking more like the son of Guy's mother than her husband.

Then there was the first pulsating throb; the walls trembled and the throbbing grew more powerful and in Gray's cabin objects began to vibrate. The ship's turbines cut in with a high-pitched howl, it was as if the *Ark Royal's* heart had commenced beating.

As the anchor chain began to rattle upwards, de Gray grabbed his cap, then flung a glance at himself in the small mirror to check if he was properly dressed. The vibrations and trembling increased. *Ark Royal* was like a thoroughbred dog ready and eager to be let off the leash.

All was hectic activity on the flight-deck. Duty pilots marched slowly from the lift leading from the ready-room to their planes. Hooded mechanics busied themselves with chocks and fuel lines, Aldis lamps clattered, deck officers ran back and forth checking the leeway on both sides as the giant carrier edged her way out into the main shipping channel, while high above on the bridge, de Gray spotted the lone figure of the captain, looking like some ancient God on high directing the activities of the petty mortals below.

* * *

“We’re well on our way now, sir,” CPO Drake’s voice reached de Gray, as the linesman at the bow was letting out the last of the mooring hawser.

“Yes,” de Gray answered, grateful for the company as suddenly he felt very lonely as he stared at the mudbanks and the cleaner line of the shingle beyond, realising suddenly that he was seeing the last of England. “What d’you think? Will we be gone long?” he asked the CPO.

Drake had to take pity on the young officer. He was only a kid, really, still wet behind the ears. “Well, sir, if this was a battlewagon it could be for years. That’s why we allus sailed in daylight in them days, with the Marines playing ‘Hearts of Oak ... Steady, boys, steady!’ and the crowds was cheering and the kids wailing and womenfolk crying.”

He grinned crookedly. “Now, we sneak out after dark like a lot of villains. *How long?* They’re allus moving carriers about — and we’ve only got six of ’em. So we could be back in a few months if things go well.”

“Thanks, Chiefie,” Gray said, flushing as usual and telling himself that he was a bloody fool. The old CPO had taken pity on him, jollying him along the best he could.

So they stood in silence, feeling the cool breeze coming in from the sea and chilling their faces as it grew stronger, with the great ship ploughing into the growing darkness. They were too wrapped up in their own thoughts, doubts, apprehensions, to note the dark smudge on the horizon, which having spotted what it had come to discover was now turning and making its way eastwards to report. Moments later there was no dark smudge, it had vanished and *Ark Royal* was alone.

Chapter Two

"Mannschaften — stillgestanden!" the hoarse, brutal command echoed and re-echoed through the big dockside shed. As one, 160 pairs of jackboots, belonging to the crews of four U-boats, crashed down on the wet tarmac with their steel-shod soles. Outside in the fiord the excited seagulls, scavenging for titbits of food from the ships' waste, fluttered into the sky in hoarse protest.

For one long moment there was silence, broken only by the chimes of the garrison clock in the town of Kiel itself. Then the U-boat captain wheeled round and threw a salute to the lean, hard-faced Admiral on the podium, decorated with the white and black cross of the old Imperial Navy. Watching, *Leutnant zur See* von der Weide felt it to be the father of all salutes.

Admiral Karl Doenitz stiffened. His arm, working as if on steel springs, snapped up to the gold-braided brim of his cap and returned the salute. Then he spoke: *"Offiziere and Soldaten der U-Boot Waffe ... Kameraden ... Guten Morgen."*

"Morgen Herr Admiral," the brave bass voices replied in unison.

Doenitz gave them his thin, wintry smile and then called for his young, fanatical U-boat men to stand at ease. They did so gratefully, for they had been standing in this freezing shed for an hour waiting for Doenitz to explain the reason for this sudden parade. The Admiral let them stamp their feet to return the circulation and slap their hands across their frozen bodies to produce a little warmth. He told himself he should be honoured to command such a fine body of young men, who were prepared to suffer grievous losses in order to bring the perfidious English to their knees, as they had done once to the Germans so cruelly in the Old War.

Finally, judging they were ready to listen, he stepped closer to the microphone and barked in his thin, reedy voice: "Germans ... comrades ... fellow sailors, I will not waste words. We do not have the time for that. From now on every minute counts. Early this morning our planes and radio-tracking service found out something of very great importance." He paused and deliberately let them wait.

Next to *Leutnant zur See* von der Weide, his neighbour growled, "Come on, old man, piss or get off the pot. I've got some hot gash waiting for me back in my quarters. I'd like to get a piece of it before I go out and die bravely for Folk, Fatherland and Fuhrer."

Kurt von der Weide grinned. They were all great, even fanatical, patriots, but they were also hot-blooded young men who knew they were going to die sooner or later and wanted to enjoy the fruits of life before they did so. "You're not the only one," he began to say, when Doenitz spoke up again.

"We have spotted the *Ark Royal!*"

That caused a buzz of excited chatter. Everyone on parade knew just how desperate the *Kriegsmarine* and Minister Josef Goebbels were to achieve the great propaganda victory of sinking Britain's most modern and greatest aircraft carrier.

"She left the southern English port of Portsmouth at dusk last night and took a south-easterly course. But that can mean nothing. Once she's well out to sea she can easily change course. At present our planes and a lone surface craft are shadowing her ready to report any change in her course. But fog is predicted for that area at about noon, so we may lose her. You know, all of you, that Fat Hermann's boys are not the most persistent of warriors when it comes to bad weather. A sharp gust and they're scurrying back to their airfields." *Reichsmarshal* Hermann Goering, head of the *Luftwaffe,* was known as 'Fat Hermann' because of his very large girth. Doenitz smiled coldly, his sally against the pilots of the *Luftwaffe* caused some laughter, they envied the luxurious kind of life the German air force enjoyed in their French bases.

"Now then, comrades," Doenitz continued hastily, while outside the huge shed the gulls dived and squawked in protest at something, "what are we of the U-boat arm going to do? Just in case

Ark Royal changes course and heads north to join their Home Fleet at Scapa Flo, all U-boats in the Belgian and Norwegian ports have been alerted for immediate action."

The Admiral paused thoughtfully, once again realising that he might be falling into that strategic dilemma that had been the ruination of many military commanders, that of dividing his forces so that he was not strong enough at any one point to force a decisive victory.

"My guess is, however, that the *Ark Royal* is heading south for the Mediterranean. I have therefore ordered our U-boat commanders at Lorient to cease all attacks on the Allied Atlantic convoys for the time being and concentrate on the Bay of Biscay area. One final matter: I have ordered the U-boat flotilla at Messina, the port on Sicily that faces Italy, to stand-down their current crews, who are all inexperienced. We must have the best out there, so in their places I am sending four of my best U-boat crews to replace them. At 1200 hours precisely these crews will be flying out by special planes from Hamburg. So there is little time to be lost."

He nodded to his elegant young adjutant with the long, golden lanyard hanging from his left shoulder. The latter stepped forward briskly to the second mike, carrying a sheaf of papers. He unfolded them and began to read: "The following skippers and their crews are to be transferred to Italy immediately: Hartmann, *Leutnant zur See ...* Jost, *Oberleutnant zur See ..."*

Eagerly, von der Weide listened for his own name, which would be last, if it was on the list at all, and he prayed that it would be. All the older skippers had cured their throat-ache, meaning that they had won the Knight's Cross of the Iron Cross, including Gunther Prien, Otto Kretschmer and the rest. Now it was the turn of the young hopefuls including himself. Indeed, his father had maintained time and time again that he should win the coveted award as soon as possible. Not that he was a fanatical Nazi; on the contrary, his father looked down his long, aristocratic nose at such upstarts. But he was also a realist. "Glory and baubles, they'll win us back our estates," he quavered all too often. "That last war ruined us, lost us our power, our cash and our estates. This war is going to have to restore the balance and to do so we need military success. My boy, we need your picture in the popular press, photos of you with the Fuehrer and the top brass, even with those working-class swine of 'Golden Pheasants'. *Our war is not for glory, but for money and possessions!"*

"Von der Weide, *Leutnant zur See."* There it was, Kurt rejoiced. He had been selected and therefore passed the first stage of the great race for 'tin' and fame, even as Doenitz returned to the microphone and announced, "This is going to mean tin for even the youngest Moses on board" — the most junior U-boat crewmen were always nicknamed 'Moses'.

A burly *Obermaat,* his barrel-chest covered in 'tin', stepped forward, pulled off his beribboned cap and bellowed in a schnapps-thickened voice, "Three cheers for the Admiral! Hip — hip — hip ..."

A great wave of cheering swept through the large shed, while Kurt's mind raced, considering the possibilities which had just been opened up to him. He knew with the perfect, total clarity of a revelation that he was going to be the one who sank the *Ark Royal.* He simply *had* to. The future of the von der Weide line depended upon it. When he was long dead and gone, some future descendant would be looking at his yellowing portrait in the gloomy gallery of Schloss Trutz von der Weide and saying proudly, "That was my ancestor who put the family back on its feet again. He died young, but he died gloriously *for the family!"*

Heated by that immense thought, his face flushed, he hardly heard Doenitz's last statement, delivered in a low, grave voice, "Dear comrades, come back victorious — like the ancient Greeks." But he hesitated slightly, then added, "... or come back on your shields — dead."

Excitedly, Kurt bounded two at a time up the stairs of the nineteenth century boarding house, hardly panting. He didn't give a fig whether Frau Arnsen on the second floor, with her damned canary and ugly dachshund, heard him or not, the nosy old bitch. Who knows, he may never come this way again. When he returned after sinking the *Ark Royal,* he'd probably be consorting with Goebbels' starlets or the prosperous daughters of big-business magnates. They all liked to be associated with the heroes of the

Thousand-Year Reich. Then he'd be adding some very attractive, French-perfumed tufts of pubic hair to those already pinned to a board nearly filled with neatly labelled souvenirs of his former conquests, which he called his Trophy Board, similar to the way his ancestors had once done with the heads of game which they had shot all over Europe.

Breathing just a little harder, he paused in front of the door with its highly polished handle and brass plate bearing the legend *'Frau Kapitanleutnant Inge Wolff verwitwet'.* He grinned. The widow of the recently killed-in-action U-boat captain had obviously not taken her 'grievous' loss too seriously and the hall smelled of lino polish and the window sparkled just like the brass plate on the door.

He pressed the bell. Inge Wolff, the new widow, opened the door at once, as if she had been expecting him. All the same, she feigned surprise. "I thought you had already gone, Kurt."

Knowing how much she liked bawdy talk, he said, "I haven't even come yet!" And when she was in the right mood sexually she liked a slap or two as well to brighten her passion.

At the moment, however, she looked attractive, but as suitably demure as the neighbours expected from a local girl who had just lost her U-boat skipper husband, fallen in the struggle for Folk, Fatherland and Fuhrer. She wore all black, setting off her blonde hair, but he noticed immediately that her stockings were not simply black cotton as was customary in bourgeoisie Kiel, but sheer black silk, obviously bought in German-occupied France, together with the usual sexy silk underwear that the delighted women were given by their husbands when they came home on leave from that country.

"I've got three hours before I fly away!" he cried and flung his cap at the hat-stand where it landed safely on a peg as it had always done in the past when he had sneaked in to see her while her husband had been at sea.

"But you can't stay here just now!" she protested.

"Why not?"

"What will the neighbours say? It's broad daylight and, besides, they'll hear," she mumbled, lowering her eyes demurely.

"Frig the neighbours!" he snorted. "And when have you ever cared about making a noise while we're making the beast with two backs and dancing the mattress polka?" he asked scornfully.

He sat down without another word and started carelessly pulling off his muddy shoes, not worrying in the slightest whether they were making a mess on her clean carpet.

"But —" he didn't let her finish, but rose and with the flat of his hand gave her a hearty shove and she fell backwards over the sofa, her legs spreading involuntarily to reveal her plump naked thighs and above them a thin wisp of black silk.

"Oh, Kurt!" she simpered, legs straight up in the air, her charms all revealed.

He stared down at her. "Yes!" he said brutally. "Very definitely 'Oh, Kurt!'"

He ripped his flies open and she could see he was already erect. Her eyes widened. "But it's only nine in the morning —" she began, but not for long. Her protest suddenly became a sigh of sharp relief as he mounted her. After that, she didn't care. Her whole being was concentrated on his thrusting back and forth ... back and forth.

They finished with a simultaneous shriek of abandoned, total joy and excitement, oblivious to the angry rattle of Frau Arnsen's pans below. She had obviously heard them and was making her annoyance clear at such disgusting 'piggery' at this time of the morning when a good *Hausfrau* should be concerned with shopping and preparing the midday meal.

Inge didn't care. She lay there, still panting, her legs spread wide as if she were willing to start all over again. He yawned and wasn't interested; satisfied for the moment. She let him doze off for a while, his blonde hair matted and sticky with sweat, and pressed his head against her yielding breasts. Finally, she ran her hand lightly round his damp face. He woke with a start the way he always did, as if he were back on active service.

"What time is it?" he asked thickly,

"You've got just over half an hour left," she answered softly, wondering why men were always in a hurry.

He reached for a cigarette. "A cancer stick first." He lit the *Juno Eckstein,* the cheap, working man's cigarette, which he preferred and smiled at her. “That was good, Inge. You did well by me.”

She nodded, but said nothing. Instead, she watched his profile in the three-winged dressing-table mirror. It was a face she had seen many times in these last three terrible years of war. It had first been her husband Lutz, then the other U-boat skippers who had sneaked into her bed after he had been posted ‘Missing, believed killed in action’. Now Kurt. Drunk or sober, desperate or calm, fanatical or cynical, each one of them had had the haunted features of men facing sudden, violent death.

Suddenly, so suddenly that he startled her, he stubbed his cigarette out and cruelly grabbed her arms. “Come on, Inge, let’s practise that sexual swinery once more. It’s the only thing worth living for after all, isn’t it!” Then he pushed her on to her back again and thrust himself into her as if it were of vital importance.

Chapter Three

"Next request by Able Seaman Dodds," CPO Drake barked at an uneasy Guy, who 'wore' his cap on the metal table because he was on duty, taking the parade of the morning 'Request men'.

Gray looked at the old CPO, who shouted: "Able Seaman Dodds ... Three paces forward — march!" Drake wondered whether the young, confused officer was ready for anything that might come on such a parade, from an errant wife to the usual sailor, found on every ship, who complained that "He tried to touch me up in the heads, sir, and I'm not having any of that, sir!"

"Able Seaman Dodds, sir!" Drake repeated, as the old sailor saluted and fixed his gaze to the left of the officer's shoulder.

"What's this about, Dodds?" Guy asked hesitantly. It was the first time in his naval career that he had had to deal with 'Request men'.

Dodds needed no urging to speak. "Pinched the end off'n me breakfast banger, sir," he announced with suppressed emotion.

"Who did?" Guy asked in bewilderment. He only half-understood the old sailor, who was a three-striper and who, as probably the oldest rating in the ship, had just been posted to the gun draft to show the others the ropes, as the young Guns, the gunnery officer, had explained.

"That friggin' Mick, if you'll excuse me French, sir. Him that calls hissen 'Sparks'." He made a contemptuous face. "Like to request a grudge fight with the big Paddy, sir." Guy looked hesitantly at Drake for guidance. The CPO nodded his head. A grudge fight was permissible. He cleared his throat, as if he had been dealing with such matters for years, and said, "Know anything about this, Chiefie?" It was an absurd question of course. Drake knew about everything that happened in his mess.

"Sir," CPO Drake was now very formal, as if this was an extremely grave matter. "It appears that Able Seaman Dodds' mess doesn't like pussers' sausages," meaning Navy issue sausages, "so they clubbed together to buy some NAAFI bangers. They've got skins and if yer get them so-called cooks to do 'em right the ends break open and they get nice and crisp. It appears that Able Seaman Dodds was particularly partial to them ends —"

"Best meal of the day, sir," the latter interjected, "if them soddin' thievin' cooks do 'em right with a bit of fried bread ..."

Drake frowned at Dodds severely and he shut up like a clam. Even in his outraged state the able seaman knew that it wasn't wise to get on the wrong side of old Drakie. "Anyway, sir, according to his own statement, Able Seaman Dodds had just turned his back to discuss the future strategy of the war — or so he sez — when Sparks bit the end off'n his banger, sir."

"Just about to treat mesen, sir, and I was gonna use me knife and not me fingers, when I turn and find the end of me NAAFI banger gorn. It ain't friggin' fair, sir."

"Quite." Guy de Gray found himself saying. "And now you want a grudge fight. But don't you realise that your opponent is twice your size and half your age?"

"Don't matter, sir," Dodds said doggedly. "He nicked the end of me banger and he's got to pay for it. I'm not having it — NAAFI sausages as well, very expensive." He glowed with self-righteousness and indignation.

Guy looked again at Drake. "Does Sparks want to fight as well, Chiefie?"

"He's a Mick, sir," as if that was explanation enough.

Guy de Gray nodded. He looked at the angry three-striper. Unless he could get Drake to have a word and get Sparks to go easy on the older man, the Mick would murder him, But Guy knew that Dodds would demand his rights come what may. He reached for his wooden pen and the Request Book. "All right, Dodds, permission for the grudge fight granted. Tomorrow at 1300 hours on the mid-deck," he snapped.

Gray was nearly deafened as, next to him, CPO Drake bellowed the same order to Dodds, ending with, "About turn ... double march ... let's look lively, now, Dodds!" The old stripey shot out, still muttering something about his precious NAAFI bangers.

By the early morning of the following day it looked as if the grudge fight might have to be cancelled. It had been anticipated by the rest of the draft as a break in the routine monotony of their daily round, but just after first light, as the first watch ate their breakfast and Dodds presumably guarded his precious bangers jealously, the alarm bells and rattles started to sound and over the Tannoy system the Marine bugler called the Stand-To, an old eighteenth century drill allied to twentieth century technology.

"It's a shad," CPO gasped as he struggled into his helmet and duffel-coat. "We've been bloody well spotted!" Even in front of the officer he couldn't hide his irritation at the knowledge.

"A what?" Guy asked, as the draft took their places behind the banked-up, massed .5 in. machine-guns and Oerlikon cannon that were now their charges.

" 'Shad' for 'shadow', young Gray," a brisk, cheerful voice answered him. It was Guns, as he had by now learned to call the Gunnery Officer, who spent as much time as he could training the raw gunnery recruits. "Presumably one of their four-engined Condors, they've got a tremendous range. The bugger has been shadowing us and reporting our movements back to their naval HQ in Paris." He frowned, "Something that we could do without this particular morning." He saw the puzzled look in the younger officer's eyes and added, "You see, we're going to change course south-east sometime this morning when it suits the captain."

The knowledge meant little to de Gray, but a lot to CPO Drake. Under his breath he cursed to himself, "Fire and brimstone — it's the Med after all. Now we're friggin' well for it!"

Now, a tense silence fell over the aft gun-deck as the men sat at their action stations, not even noticing the biting cold as they watched the tiny black spot of the German reconnaissance plane fly round and round, too far away for its engines to be heard.

After what seemed an age, the Aldis lamp above them on the bridge started to clatter. Guy de Gray turned to Bunts in bewilderment, "What are we sending the bugger, Bunts?" It was obvious that the signals yeoman could only be sending to the 'shad'.

Bunts puffed out his chest, proud to have been selected as the only specialist among the draft. "I sent: 'FROM THE CAPTAIN: CAN YOU FLY ROUND THE OTHER WAY. YOU ARE MAKING ME DIZZY'."

Guy grinned in spite of his inner tension and CPO Drake commented, "Bit of a card, the skipper, sir!"

A few moments later they knew the unknown German pilot also had a sense of humour. In clear English he signalled: 'ANYTHING TO OBLIGE AN ENGLISHMAN' then the Condor broke off to starboard and started to make lazy circles in the opposite direction.

"Thought the Jerries didn't have a ruddy sense of humour?" Bunts commented, his moment of glory over.

The morning passed at a snail's pace, with no one on the gun-platforms able to take their eyes off the 'shad' for more than a second or two. Then the cold started to intensify. It gripped their bodies with icy fingers and even when they stamped their seaboots on the frosty deck their feet seemed without life. It was as if Nature was numbing them before whatever terrible surprise Man had in store for them.

"We're a friggin' aircraft carrier," Sparks said angrily. "Aircraft means aeroplanes. So why ain't we sending up aeroplanes to knock the Jerry basket out of the sky?" Bunts had no answer.

Guy de Gray grinned. He had already learned in his short service career that whenever a matelot stopped grumbling there was trouble coming. They were still moaning 'stinking fish', as CPO Drake called it, so they were still up to the mark, whatever was to come soon.

In the end they gave up on the 'shad'. Although lookouts were posted to keep an eye on the German plane circling on the horizon, too high for the *Ark's* aircraft and out of range of the guns, the majority of the crew went about their normal duties, glad to be moving and driving the freezing air from their stiff limbs, and cadging hot drinks whenever they could, waiting for the first cry of 'Splice the mainbrace', when they could swallow a stiff tot of heart-warming rum.

At 1300, after sandwiches of semi-frozen bully beef and already stale ship's bread (when the 'shad' had been first sighted the galley fires had been dowsed ready for action, so no bread had been baked for the day), those of the draft who were off duty assembled for the grudge fight between the diminutive Dodds and the big, handsome young Irishman. Both of them, kitted out with proper boxing gloves and stripped down to singlets and shorts according to King's Regulations, were blue with cold.

"Now then," CPO Drake warned the two of them, while the spectators stamped their feet and blew into their gloves, "you both know the rules. Carry on fighting until one of you has had enough. After it's all over you will shake hands and I want no more quarrelling or you'll be run in before yer ruddy plates of meat can bloody well touch the deck. All right?"

The two faced each other; the old three-striper with his over-large false teeth, and the young, big Irishman who by his expression seemed to be regretting that he had ever accepted the other man's challenge. The stripey was obviously going to be the loser, but he was the type who would take a lot of stick before he gave in. His kind had been used to taking knocks all their lives.

Warily, the Irishman circled the stripey, who struck an old-fashioned pose like one of those nineteenth century bare-knuckle fighters, chin stuck out invitingly, waiting for the fight to come to him.

"Come on, Paddy, get stuck in!" the crowd encouraged the younger man, hoping for some action to relieve the boredom of the afternoon. "Give him the old one-two!"

But silently the Irishman mouthed "Fuck off!" while the stripey grinned, obviously thinking that the younger man was afraid of him.

Guy shook his head while next to him a watchful CPO Drake said, *sotto voce,* "There's fools like that three-striper born every bloody minute. You wait and see. The Mick'll wipe the deck with him in a mi —"

He never finished. Suddenly, while the Irishman danced round him, fists held loose, the old matelot reached out and hit the unwary Mick right on his nose. The latter yelped with pain and staggered back, moaning thickly, "The sod's gone and hit me on the hooter!" He certainly had, and blood started to pour from the Irishman's injured nostrils and trickle down his chin to drop off and colour his singlet.

One of the onlookers laughed, "Old stripey's gorn and tapped his friggin' claret, wonders'll never cease!"

Dodds, proud of the success of his surprise attack, pranced about in a heavy-footed manner, making jabs through the air at an imaginary opponent, but not for long. Abruptly, an enraged Sparks flung himself forward, fists flailing. He caught Dodds completely off guard and the man reeled backwards, livid red patches appearing on his face.

"Hey!" he called in protest, "That wasn't fair! You didn't tell me you were gonna hit me, you bloody Mick!" and with great delight the spectators took up the chant, "Tell him when yer gonna hit 'im, Paddy! It's only fair, mate!"

The Irishman lashed out again. The blow glanced off Dodds' chin. His false teeth hung out of his mouth stupidly and while trying to push them back he defended himself the best he could with the other hand. He staggered back again, still fiddling with those false teeth, while the Mick, breathing hard, paused and prepared to launch the knock-out blow at Dodds. But it was not to be.

Several things happened as Sparks pulled his right arm back to strike. The alarm klaxons began to sound their urgent warning. The ready pilots emerged onto the swaying flight-deck and raced across it as hooded mechanics scrambled to start the engines of the aircraft. Below the bridge, Guns was shouting angrily, his face red and furious, "Back to your guns ... back to your guns, for Christ's sake! ... it's an attack!"

CPO Drake spun round with surprising speed for a man of his years. He gasped, there was no mistaking it. Out of nowhere a small vessel had appeared. But it was not the fishing-boat which caught his eye, it was the dark, sinister outline of the craft wallowing in the troughs beyond it.

Then he scrambled to the gun-platform, yelling over his shoulder, "What d'yer friggin' well want, written permission? IT'S A FRIGGIN' JERRY U-BOAT!"

And far down in the bowels of the *Ark Royal,* clustered together with the ratings, sweat glistening on their furrowed foreheads, listening to the *ping-ping-ping* of the asdic, the operator staring at the flickering green screen of the radar grabbed quickly for the phone to the bridge.

"Bridge ... bridge!" he shouted, all standard operating procedure forgotten for the moment. *"The sub's launched a torpedo!"*

Chapter Four

As the first of the Fairey Fulmar fighters hurtled down the flight-deck, with the deck crew praying that nothing would go wrong at this most dangerous moment of the launch, Guy de Gray's inexperienced gun-crews opened up for the first time. The situation out to port was confused, the U-boat wallowing there, long, black and sinister,

To her almost immediate front was the most ancient coal-burner leaving a thick cloud of black smoke, nigh on impenetrable in places, trailing behind her from the single stack. An angry, frustrated CPO Drake didn't know whether the little boat was a decoy for the submarine or whether she had been there just by chance. But what he did know was that she was a bloody nuisance and getting in the way of accurate shooting as the trainee gunners lowered their barrels as far as they could and peppered the sea all round the U-boat.

High above them on the bridge, the god-like figure of the captain was issuing a string of orders, fervently trying to bring the *Ark Royal* round and out of the path of the tin fish. Had he a moment, CPO Drake would have prayed for the captain's success but he was too busy. There was much to do on the gun-platform.

Guns came clattering down the companion-way from the bridge, yelling, "Hose the sea in front of that bloody freighter or whatever the hell she is. We might knock the tin fish out if we're lucky," his voice striving to be heard above the metallic din of thousands of empty brass cartridge cases tumbling to the deck.

He stared to port. The air was streaked with a mass of flying tracer, glowing white and zigzagging wildly. Shells exploded round the strange ship, raising huge spouts of white water to her port and starboard sides. The first of the Fulmars was dropping out of the sky towards the U-boat sheltering in the lee of the freighter, its machine-guns chattering.

The U-boat would soon crash-dive to escape the approaching danger, but Guns did not care about that, he was concerned with those torpedoes heading in their direction at a deflection angle. It would be a matter of moments now before the *Ark Royal* was hit.

Guns' train of thought was suddenly shattered by a great hollow boom of steel striking steel. In two halves from amidships, the freighter seemed to leap partly out of the water. Guns opened his mouth instinctively to prevent his eardrums from being broken. A shock-wave slapped him across the face and the air was nearly dragged from his lungs and he blinked and gasped like an asthmatic.

In a flash what was left of the freighter burst into bright, scarlet flame as she began to founder. Great searing flames shot the length of the broken deck as if from a giant blowtorch. In front of the horrified eyes of the British matelots on the decks of the carrier they saw sailors, already ablaze, panicking and running to the rails, flinging themselves into the icy sea below. One man had climbed the mast, then he dived off, but misjudged the distance and slammed into the deck, every bone in his body broken. Other members of the doomed crew ran to and fro like chickens, unable to make a life-saving decision as seawater started to wash about their feet and the end grew closer.

The pilot of the second Fulmar had no eyes for the tragedy taking place on the sinking freighter. His gaze was concentrated solely on the U-boat, now exposed, its cover gone. The fighter came in at sea-top level, machine-guns blazing. Ruthlessly, the pilot raked the diving U-boat's superstructure.

"Cease firing!" yelled Guns above the tremendous noise. *"Cease firing!"* and reluctantly, motivated solely by the desire to kill, the draft did so. Gun after gun fell silent as the Fulmar banked and came in once more, showing no mercy for the obviously doomed submarine. Its bridge was littered with dead German sailors and it circled out of control, offering the pilot easy gun practice. He poured down a tremendous volume of fire, hosing the U-boat from end to end. Then he ran out of ammo and turned away.

Slowly at first, motivated more by a feeling of relief and wonder than triumph, cheering began on *Ark Royal,* growing by the instant until the sound drowned the ship's turbine. They were saved, they had done their bit — they had destroyed the enemy that came from below.

"Five to ten minutes at the most," the remote figure of the captain high above them on the bridge had ordered. Now, the *Ark Royal's* engines were running softly, as her aircraft warily circled the scene on the lookout for trouble, while her crew picked up the survivors. "Only the ones that look alive," Guns had insisted curtly. "No time for the possibles — too bloody dangerous. The Jerries don't care, they'd stick a torpedo up our arse whatever the circumstances."

Horrified and mesmerised at the same time, Guy de Gray watched as members of his draft stood by with oars and boathooks, scanning the dead or possibly unconscious men as they drifted past the hull, ready to scoop out only those who looked as if they had a chance. So this is war, Guy told himself, sickened by it all but forcing himself to look all the same. It was nothing like those heroic paintings he had been brought up with: officers in smart uniforms, surrounded by admiring ordinary erks, dying gallantly in the arms of some brave young ensign, the flags fluttering bravely in the background, with the red-cheeked drummer-boy preparing to play a last roll of honour on his side-drum.

Those men in the water were dying horribly, coughing out their oil-choked lungs, pleading with God, who this terrible day was looking the other way. As they thrashed feebly in the waves they moaned for mothers who would never hear their cries.

"More survivors, sir," Sparks said, hardly able to conceal the horror in his voice. "Down there."

Guy craned his neck to see over the gun parapet and next instant wished he hadn't. A matelot was trying to pull up a fat sailor. The man was screaming with pain in a language that Guy did not recognise. Suddenly the matelot lost his grip of the fat man's wrists, who fell back into the water, his screaming intensified. The sailor was left holding what seemed to be two gloves made of some red material. He had pulled the flesh right off the dying survivor's hands and wrists, and he began to retch. There was nothing more to be done as in the sea below the man's struggles became weaker, until he finally gave up and lay still, slowly sinking beneath the surface, his arms waving as he awaited the benison of death.

But even now, in the middle of this mission of mercy, there was no let-up from the grim, cruel brutality of war. Suddenly, the rescuers' ears were assailed by the roar of engines. Klaxons shrilled their urgent warning. Guy de Gray flashed a look upwards, seeing a twin-engined Ju 88 streaking in at mast-top height.

Almost immediately the guns took up the challenge with flashes of angry cherry-red flame spurting from their muzzles. Brown and grey puff-balls of smoke exploded all round the German bomber but it seemed to bear a charmed life as it weaved through the ack-ack fire. Still the pilot pressed home his bold attack — then his plane seemed to stagger momentarily as it released its 6,000 lb bomb load in a stick of six. Then the Ju 88 was soaring high into the air, revealing the length of its underside. Guy could see the oil streaks on the wings behind the two engines.

The bombs hit the wash on both sides of the aircraft carrier. They were so close that *Ark Royal* shivered and trembled as water-spouts shot up as high as the bridge.

Next moment the Ju 88 was hit. The pilot must have been killed outright for one moment the bomber was climbing steadily and the next it was falling out of the sky, leaving a trail of smoke. It hit the water in a great, whirling spout and went straight under. Neither the pilot nor the observer got out and on *Ark Royal* no one cheered. Her crew were too saddened and depressed by the death and destruction they had seen.

Five minutes later, CPO Drake asked quietly if he would follow him and they went to where some of the draft, those who had been stood down and were off duty, gazed upwards, white-faced. "Make way, lads," Drake said in a subdued voice for him, "I want to show the officer something ... make way there."

Silent and subdued, the men did so. Guy de Gray looked up and was horrified when he saw what Drake had to show him. It was Dodds, the old three-striper, perched high on the lookout cage, his head dangling so that his large, yellowed, Hassler false teeth were hanging half-out of his gaping mouth. His body had been riddled by machine-gun fire from the German aircraft as it made its pass across the carrier's deck. He could not have survived that attack, and there was still the frightening, steady drip, drip of blood coming from the body to indicate that Dodds had lived, addicted to his simple liking of those NAAFI bangers.

Next to him, Mick, the big Irishman who had won the grudge fight, crossed himself and whispered, "Jesus, son of Mary ... you poor old bastard!"

Guy closed his eyes and fought back the bitter-tasting bile which threatened to choke him.

Drake took his arm and said quietly, "I'll get somebody to tend to him, sir." He guessed what de Gray was going through. "Don't worry yer head about him. I'll see he's laid to rest all ship-shape and Bristol fashion. He would have wanted that, poor old git."

"Thanks, Chiefie, I appreciate that," Guy said. "You know, Dodds is the first dead person I've ever seen."

Drake said nothing, but he told himself that before this little lot was over the young sub-lieutenant would see a lot more dead men — if he lived long enough himself. So he went away without another word, while the draft still stared upwards at the body swaying slightly as the *Ark Royal* got under way once more. They waited in silence for the burial party to arrive, still hearing the drip, drip of Dodds' blood.

Half an hour later they buried him. Guns had informed Guy that the Captain would be unable to attend. The ship was closing the Bay of Biscay and he had major problems to worry about. So it became Guy's job to supervise the sail-maker as he sewed the corpse up in a length of canvas. It wasn't a job Guy wanted to do, but he knew that he had to do it. He stuck it out until the very last, when the sail-maker, squatting cross-legged on deck like a tailor, had almost closed the shroud and then, as a kind of afterthought, thrust his large curved needle through Dodds' tongue. Guy winced. He had heard about it, and knew why it was done, but never thought he would ever see it. It dated back to the days of Nelson and was a check to make sure the supposed corpse was really dead and not shamming. Dodds was really dead and, satisfied, the sail-maker added the last stitch.

A few minutes later Guns had read the excerpt from the burial service, muttered a few hurried words about 'our dead but dearly beloved shipmate', then Dodds went over the side, forgotten almost before his corpse hit the waves. He had been the usual reliable, tolerant, conservative stripey, who had known all the tricks of his trade and all the dodges of naval life from Pompey Hard to the Persian Gulf. Now he'd gone and no one mourned him, while someone else would scoff the rest of his NAAFI bangers.

Chapter Five

"Maintenant, je vais chanter!" shrieked the drunken, near-nude blonde — who wasn't a blonde at all, which was obvious — *"jetzt werde ich singen!"* She looked dizzily at the officers who crowded the smoke-filled room and nearly fell off the platform where the whores sometimes danced with their clients, those of whom could stay on their feet.

Behind her, the drummer, a cigarette glued to his bottom lip, said scornfully to the bored accordion player who was idly scratching his crotch, *"Sale con ... sale con'un boche."*

The accordionist yawned, totally disinterested.

Von der Weide, who knew some French from his time at the German U-boat base in the occupied port of Lorient, noted the anti-German sentiment routinely but he had not the slightest interest in what the decadent French thought about their German occupiers. The Frogs had been well and truly beaten, so historically and individually they no longer existed for him.

Due to engine trouble, Kurt von der Weide had had to force-land here at Lyon, and every minute counted if *he* were going to sink the *Ark Royal.* It was a nuisance, but there were worse places to waste a night. French brothels were pretty good if a man didn't get too drunk, and he usually got good value for his money. Since the drunken blonde who wasn't a true blonde had taken over — she was an Alsatian and spoke German as her native tongue — things had gone smoothly and the U-boat officers had virtually taken over the whorehouse. This did not particularly please the French, who were in the majority, many of whom wore the tainted uniform of Vichy France.

But again, what *they* thought did not matter a fig to von der Weide. Let them sulk and posture and mutter sullenly beneath their drink-smelling breath. They had had their chance and had been well and truly beaten.

The blonde, staggering dangerously, dressed in nothing but black silk panties and, for some reason known only to herself, in a pair of sea-officer's leather deck-boots, pushed her way past the drunken U-boat officers and on to the little elevated dance-floor. Greedy hands reached out to twitch her pert buttocks, and 'Hamburg Willi', an old hare whom some had said hadn't been sober since 1939 when war had been declared, yelled, "Get a load of that rigging she's got on her ... Could use that better than for singing. Yer could bury yer head between those tits and know no pain for a couple of weeks!"

His supposed witticism was met by a burst of drunken laughter from *Kapitan-leutnant* van de Dat, the flotilla's only remaining ace, an officer whom von der Weide disliked intensely. After all, he had 'cured his throat-ache' and vain as the Commander was he had even had postcards of himself printed which he gave to pretty girls. Now, de Dat lifted his head from between the breasts of the naked whore sitting on his lap, took a swig of stale beer, then disliked the taste and spat the frothy liquid into the nearest vase of flowers, which immediately began to wilt.

"Let's have a bit of order and discipline — *German discipline* — in this knocking-shop!" van de Dat ordered as the senior officer present. "Let the cowbag sing and then it's up the cups, gentlemen, and get in there, Uncle Otto, before it gets cold!" He laughed drunkenly.

Opposite, a young French naval officer, wearing the gold badge of the submarine service on his tunic, looked angry, he obviously understood German, and farted contemptuously. No one else heard, they were too drunk, but von der Weide did and he didn't give a damn what the French submariner thought. Idly, a little smile on his lips, he was wondering what Admiral Doenitz would have thought if he had known just how his picked U-boat officers were celebrating their first night on French soil before they set out from Sicily on their vital mission.

By now up on the stage, the drunken whore was warbling a popular French love-song but well out of tune, her ample breasts wobbling delightfully every time she reached a high note. But love was furthest from the U-boat officers' minds. "Take yer drawers off!" they bellowed in red-faced lechery. "By the great whore of Buxtehude, can't yer sing anything else than that Frog trash?" A naked ensign climbed onto the stage and wagged his skinny bare buttocks to cheers and laughter.

While the Frenchmen grew progressively more sombre and sullen-looking, especially the officers, the German U-boat men grew wilder and wilder, shouting at the tops of their voices and throwing anything that came to hand. Drunk as she was, the Alsatian whore knew she had to do something before the place was wrecked. She knew these young men in uniform, they were doomed to live short, brutish lives and didn't care much about the consequences of their actions. She swung round dizzily and snapped to the band, *"Allez vite ... Horst Wessel Lied!"*

Completely off-key the two musicians started to play the infamous Nazi Party marching song and the girl sprang into action at once. Right hand raised in the party salute, she began goose-stepping up and down the stage, singing lustily, *"Die fahn hoch ... die Reihen fest gerschlosser ... SA marschiert in gleichen, festen Schritt!"*

The French reacted at once. There was angry murmuring that quickly changed into booing and shrill whistling and fists being shaken at the beery Germans. The young French submariner reached threateningly for his pistol but an older comrade grabbed his arm and forced him to replace the gun in its holster. The smoke-filled air was thick with resentment and sheer, naked hate.

Von der Weide felt no part of it all. Let them play their silly patriotic games, he told himself. Being wise beyond his years, in essence it was, he knew, nothing to do with national pride; it was nothing more than sexual envy.

As if reacting to von der Weide's theory, the French submarine officer picked up a bottle of expensive champagne from his table, held it by the neck and cursing angrily at *'les salauds'* threw it at Hamburg Willi. He missed the old hare and instead the bottle shattered on the naked ensign's flabby buttocks and he yelped with surprised pain, crying, "I think he's gone and cut off me friggin' eggs! I'm a eunuch, comrades, I'll never shag again!"

That did it. Hamburg Willi lurched to his feet. "Arse with ears!" he roared at the young French officer and launched himself in a wild dive, fists like small steam-shovels ready for the fray. Next moment he had slammed them into the Frenchman's face and the handsome features spattered gorily in a welter of blood through which his teeth glistened like polished ivory, as he went flying over the back of his chair.

On the raised platform, the drunken blonde wet herself while crying in desperation, *"Non! ... non! ... Meine Herren — nich, ich bitte Sie!"* But no one was listening to her as the room erupted into violence. Glasses flew through the air, chairs shattered, tables went skidding across the floor. On the stage the two musicians who had played on valiantly for a while gave up as a flower-vase crashed to pieces against the wall by their heads, drenching them in foul-smelling water. They fled for cover.

Von der Weide ducked another missile and knew that it was going to get worse and had no intention of becoming involved in the stupid, mindless brawl. "I've come here to fuck!" he snarled to himself, "and I will!" He flung a hasty glance round the chaotic scene, looking for the whores. But, wise to the ways of drunken seamen, they had fled through the rear door, all save the Alsatian girl who swayed to and fro on the debris-littered stage, looking down very seriously at her soiled panties as if wondering what had caused her little accident.

Von der Weide did not give her the chance to find out. He sprang to his feet and a waiter tried to bar his way, waving his arms in what he thought was a fighting manner. Von der Weide laughed. That wasn't the way he fought. His right foot lashed out and it caught the waiter between the legs. The man gagged with surprise and pain, his false teeth bulging stupidly from a gaping mouth. All von der Weide needed to do was give him a gentle push and he reeled backwards to the floor. Von der Weide leaped over him and climbed up on to the stage, narrowly dodging a bottle aimed at him. In her drunken state, the girl blinked at him.

"Hand!" von der Weide bellowed above the racket.

Obediently she did so, tripping over her panties, which were halfway down her shapely legs. He tugged the girl down off the stage, and a French civilian, his face fat with good living on the black market, tried to stop him, crying something about the *"gloire de France."*

"Fuck your gloire de France!" Kurt von der Weide snarled and punched the man viciously on the nose. The Frenchman's gold-rimmed spectacles shattered and, blinded from trying to pull the glass splinters from his face, he sat down abruptly on the beer-puddled floor.

"Los," von der Weide commanded the girl. *"Wir hauen ab."*

"Ja ... ja," she agreed.

From far off he could hear the shrill sirens of French police vans. No doubt someone had telephoned for them. *"Les flics!"* she gasped, obviously afraid. "They don't like us Alsatians, they'd put us behind Swedish curtains," holding up fingers to indicate prison bars.

He indicated that he understood. But there was no use trying to escape through the main entrance to the brothel. He dragged her to the left, while all the time the Alsatian whore tried to pull her panties up. He saw a sign 'Cloakroom' and pointed. "In here," he commanded.

He pushed her inside the dimly lit room, slammed and locked the door behind them, and then taking her by the hand led her to the rear, removing coats from their pegs as he did so. Finally he found the place he sought, a dim corner, hardly illuminated by the shadeless, fly-blown bulb. He threw the coats down and shoved her gently on top of them. She had finally managed to remove the skimpy knickers and now snuggled down comfortably with him. He pulled some coats on top of them as they heard the fight in the brothel was reaching its climax, the shrill blasts of the police whistles getting louder as the officers climbed up the stairs, panting, ordering and shouting threats.

Von der Weide felt for her breasts, big and soft like puddings. She shivered and he felt a thrill of sexual excitement spread through him. It was 24 hours since he had made love to Inge in Kiel. A soft stomach pressed against his. "Naughty!" she hissed as the police ran about close by. "Naughty boy! *Tu est très méchant!"*

Then her mouth closed over him and he held her head in his hands, surrendering to the sensation in all its delight.

It was thus while so pleasurably engaged, knowing that he could enjoy the delights offered by the drunken, yet *very* enthusiastic young whore, who was working at her chosen performance with all that thoroughness for which the Alsatians are renowned, that he became vaguely aware of the radio.

It seemed to take a very long time in getting through to his consciousness, but understandable under the circumstances of what was going on in that little cloakroom. Finally it came through and he heard that well-known bombastic fanfare, followed by the thrilled, excited voice proclaiming, *"Das Oberkommando der Wehrmacht gibt bekannt!"*

It was the radio broadcast of the High Command in Berlin, from whence the Greater German General Staff usually announced their major victories. Von der Weide's ears pricked up, but he was caught in a quandary in a manner rare to him, as the girl's mouth worked away on him as if it were the source of the greatest sexual delight and he wondered whether he should stop her. For some reason, he did not know why, he felt that the announcement had something to do with him.

Then, after the final blare of brass and rattle of kettledrums had subsided, the announcement came through. *"Early today our U-boat fleet attacked the English aircraft carrier* Ark Royal, *pride of the plutocratic Jew Winston Churchill, the tool of the capitalist world Jewry."*

He tensed and the whore, suspecting that this was the moment of his climax, redoubled her efforts, snorting like a wild animal as she worked on him.

"The English craft," the triumphant, high-pitched voice continued, "suffered major damage. However, due to a mishap in which a Belgian trawler got within the firing range of our vessels, a German U-boat was lost and the attack on the English aircraft carrier was called off. A spokesman for Admiral Doenitz, head of the German U-Boat Weapon, stated earlier today that the end of the *Ark Royal* is in sight."

Next moment, von der Weide exploded with passion, all else forgotten. He had the chance to 'cure the throat-ache' and sink the *Ark Royal* as well.

Chapter Six

Slowly the little train chugged its way along the coastline toward the new French frontier with Germany's ally Italy, trailing a black cloud of wood-smoke behind it, coal being in desperately short supply in German-occupied France.

For the most part, the U-boat men, lazing in the first-class section, leafing through *La Vie Parisienne* or other more pornographic magazines, were still hung-over from the previous night's carousal and took no notice of the land through which they passed. Von der Weide was the exception. He was now glad that the head of the German Control Commission had ordered the drunken U-boat men not to wait for their plane to be repaired, but to take the next train from Lyon to the south: that way the sensitivities of the French would no longer be aroused by their presence. The local French *prefect,* who had been present at the meeting, had agreed heartily. Again, it was a question of the *honneur* and *le Gloire.*

As he sat in his corner admiring the rich, luxuriant scenery and the fine crops of the area, mellow and prolific in the autumn sunshine, Kurt smiled at the look of indignation and outrage on the fat French official's face as he had pronounced the words which came so readily to French lips now that German arms and defeat had reduced them to the level of a fourth-class nation. Von der Weide told himself that in the years to come, covered by the blanket terms already being used by the 'Poison Dwarf', Goebbels in Berlin, of 'European Integration,' France would become little better than a German colony which would be ruled by a hand in a velvet glove, but the hand inside that glove would be made of Krupp steel.

Von der Weide stared at the rich brown soil, which needed nothing but water to make the seeds sown in it flourish so generously, and compared it with the poor East Prussian soil of his family's rundown estate. What enormous effort had to be put into it in order to produce a poor crop of potatoes or turnips, mostly fit only for his father's handful of scrawny Holstein cows. Here in France everything seemed to grow, even exotic vegetables and fruits.

One day, he told himself, when France was completely under Germany's thumb and there was peace again, perhaps the Fuhrer, as he was already doing with his victorious generals in the East, would award deserving members of the armed forces great tracts of land, turning the second-class citizens who now farmed them into humble, hard-working peasants who would be glad of a crust and a glass of cheap local wine to sustain them by way of payment. It was an exciting thought, one that could motivate a man to fight as hard as he could for his Fatherland in order to achieve that aim — and to survive.

He didn't want to be another 'Express Erickson', so called because his U-boat had destroyed an enemy express train off coastal waters. He was now dead, killed in the last attack on the *Ark Royal,* something which von der Weide had found out just before they had left Lyon Station. It had been this news that had occasioned another round of drinks and the usual cynical toasts of "Do you want to live forever, you dogs?" and "Do your best, shipmates, and if you do have to go for the chop, make a frigging handsome corpse!"

He had repeated those cruel sayings with the rest, but he had no intention of making a handsome corpse — just yet. "No, sir," he said, talking to himself as lonely men do. The war was the last chance for the von der Weide family and he had to make the most of it. He took his mind off the rich countryside, stretching right down from the mountains to the coast, and forced himself to think about the enemy and his intentions; for, as he had always told himself since the war had started, it was a wiser soldier who put himself in the place of the enemy and tried to out-guess him. It gave him the advantage.

By now he assumed, the *Ark Royal* would be well inside the Bay of Biscay and according to the latest weather forecast they had been given just before they had left Lyon 'in disgrace', as the

German Control Commission had thundered, glaring at them as if they were the lowest form of animal life, storms were forecast there, as usual. But these storms were to be accompanied by freezing fog, something to do with the French *mistral* and the Italian *tramontana.*

He shrugged a little angrily. He did not need to know the cause of bad weather, all he needed to know was its effect on operations. It was clear that due to the weather aircraft would be grounded on both sides. Naturally, both friend and foe would employ radar, but he suspected that the Germans would not attempt to direct a U-boat at the *Ark Royal* on the strength of a vague radar identification. There had already been one German failure which undoubtedly the Tommies would be telling the world about to bolster up their image of that carrier as the 'unsinkable eyes of the Royal Navy'. This time, any attack on the Tommy ship would have to be a certainty.

The thought that the *Ark Royal* would get through the Bay of Biscay safely cheered him up surprisingly. It meant that after all he would have a chance in the Mediterranean. And there in that inland sea, with German and Axis lookout posts and radar stations on both side of the Med, there was much more chance of success.

Leaning back in his seat he looked at his reflection in the carriage window. He seemed pleased, like a man who knew he was going to succeed, and raised an imaginary glass of something to himself, whispering under his breath. The toast was meant to be cynical, even comical, but at that moment it symbolised his feelings about the immediate future: *'Heil dir im Siegeskranz* — Hail thee in the victor's laurels!' Then he closed his eyes and tried to sleep. There was a busy time ahead and he'd need all his strength and stamina, but sleep would not come, his mind was too full of the great victory to come.

"Jane's got her bra off agen," Bunts said as he slumped over the dirty mess-table, trying to keep his balance as the great carrier ploughed through the heavy seas of the Bay of Biscay 200 miles away from where von der Weide tried to sleep and dream his dreams of greatness. "That girl seems to have got bigger tits than ever!"

"That's something at least," Sparks said without showing too much interest. He poked his head from beneath the rough grey Navy issue blanket which he had rolled about him like a Red Indian brave. The temperature had fallen considerably since dawn when they had entered the bay. "That cheers a bloke up on this ruddy kind of day!"

"Cheer him up more if she'd take her knickers off," someone muttered grumpily. "It's so long since I had a bit of the other that I've forgotten what it looks like. That ruddy *Daily Mirror,"* he indicated the three-day-old tabloid in Bunts' hands, "is supposed to be on the side of the lower deck matelot, so why don't they do something for us?"

"Talk," Bunts said scornfully. "Wet behind yer ears, mate, you are, if you believe that guff that comes out of London. I mean, it's the nobs what publish the *Mirror* as well, yer know. They're just in it for the old doh-ray-mi." He hawked noisily and spat on the greasy metal deck.

"Dirty bugger," a sailor said. "This deck ain't yer own front-room, yer know, Bunts." The other man lowered his paper and said quietly, "Want to make something of it, Four-eyes?"

"Yes, I do," Drake's well-known voice cut harshly into the conversation. "Off that bench, smartish. And you, remove that blanket, you look like friggin' Old Mother friggin' Riley. What a shower of shit you lot are ... and the officer doing his rounds in five minutes."

"With the Captain?" Bunts asked apprehensively as he set about removing the half-filled jam-pot that someone had somehow started to use as an ashtray.

"The Captain?" Drake echoed scornfully. "The skipper's a gent. It'd turn his delicate gent's stomach even to see a pigsty like this friggin' shambles." He sighed noisily like a man sorely tried. "Talking about pigs in shit —" Just then he heard the sound of footsteps in the companion-way and stopped speaking. Then he saw Guy de Gray and barked, "Stand by yer bunks ... officer doing the rounds!"

Blushing still as always, Guy acknowledged the CPO's salute, trying not to breathe in the fetid odour of unwashed bodies, stale cooked food and the stench of urine coming from the heads.

"Stand 'em at ease, Chiefie," he said and for a moment he paused there, taking in the scene.

It was a long narrow space, with sweating steel walls, lit by the weak yellow light of a naked electric light and the gaps in the stove that the draft had obtained illegally from somewhere — 'swopped' as they would have said. Guy's gaze fell on the dirty steel table that ran the length of the living space, their quarters, with their hammocks slung on either side. He wrinkled his nose at the sight. It was littered with dirty enamel plates, half-empty cups of cold tea and a loaf of bread covered with oily fingerprints.

He overcame his disgust at the sight and decided that he must play the officer. After all, the men expected it. To be frank, his heart went out to them, they lived under these awful conditions, boys not much older than himself, with a miserable, under-privileged past and little prospect of a better future, for less than a pound a week. Still, he knew his duty. He feigned sternness, "Bit wasteful, Chiefie, isn't it?" he said, pointing to the oil-stained loaf of bread. "With weather like this the skipper should order the galleys closed and we could be on biscuits until we reach Gib, if that's where were going."

"Exactly, sir," Drake agreed. "The next time this happens," he raised his voice for the benefit of the crestfallen draft, "I shall start taking names, then somebody'll be in for a rollocking!" He turned to Guy, who nodded his approval at the old petty officer's stern tone. "Better see the heads next, sir," he suggested.

"Do you think it necessary, Chiefie?"

"Yessir. Yer never know when the Captain might just turn up. He's very keen on heads, sir," Drake lied. It was his guess that the skipper, high above them as usual on the carrier's bridge, didn't even know the place or the men in it existed. Why, he'd only seen the captain once himself and the former had passed him by without a second look, as if he were an insignificant, ordinary seaman, not one of *Ark Royal's* most senior petty officers. Oh, yes, the Captain lived in a different world from the rest of them.

Ceremoniously they passed through the two rigid lines of matelots towards the stinking cubicles located in the gloom towards the rear. "Real lays," Drake announced.

"Yes, I can smell 'em, Chiefie. They are a bit high, aren't they!" Drake didn't answer and Guy stared around at the wads of torn *Daily Mirrors* attached to a screw, and the crude drawings of men and women engaged in sexual intercourse scribbled on the walls by constipated sailors. The written advice included, *'This ruddy roundhouse is no good at all, the seat's too big and the hole's too small.'* Beneath this another, neater hand had written, *'To which I must add this obnoxious retort; your arse is too large and your legs too short,'* while another read, *You'll have to stand up on this seat, the friggin ' crabs can jump six feet!'*

Guy tried to prevent himself laughing at the scribble, but failed. He laughed out loud, but Drake frowned. The young officer must not let himself down in front of the draft. They were already beginning to smile. Soon they'd be taking liberties. "Wipe them smiles off yer kissers, at the double!" he shouted, "Or yer feet won't touch the deck!" The smile froze on Guy's face. Again he felt inadequate. Would he never be able to do something right? It was then that CPO Drake came closer. Out of the side of his mouth he whispered, while the draft watched him with apprehension, "Suggest you keep on top of 'em, sir."

"How do you mean?"

"Well, sir, if yer average matelot doesn't get off on the right foot he's ruined forever. The bloke gets sloppy and bolshie. Seen it happen a score of times."

"I see. But what do you suggest, Chiefie?"

"PT"

"PT!" de Gray exclaimed in surprise. "But it's freezing cold out on the gun-platform. Besides, this is the off-duty watch. They'll say it's unfair!"

CPO Drake looked pityingly at the young, red-faced officer. "Hard cheese, sir. If they can't keep their quarters clean and want to live like pigs in shit, if you'll pardon the expression, sir, they'll have to learn the hard way. They won't do it agen. Tell 'em it's tough titty and make 'em get on with it. It's the only way, sir," he added, a note of false resignation in his voice as if it pained him greatly to have to suggest it.

"Oh, all right. But they don't need to put on their PT gear, not in this weather."

"As you wish, sir." CPO Drake answered. "But if you want my opinion, sir, you're spoiling 'em rotten." And with that he began shouting his orders to a very surprised draft.

Five minutes later the disgruntled draft were outside on the wind-swept gun-platform. They grumbled and groaned without a joke between them. Guy looked at the matelots, huddled in their dirty duffel-coats and slopping back and forth in their sea-boots as they attempted to stay upright, with icy raindrops slashing at their purple faces. To him they looked the most unlikely PT squad ever to confront an instructor, but later he was very glad that he had allowed them to keep their foul-weather gear on instead of changing into plimsolls, shorts and vests.

"We're just going to try a few light exercises to limber up!" he yelled, the howling wind snatching the words from his mouth. "Then you can go back to your — er — fug." He coloured at the word.

"Aye, fug it is!" someone moaned, but he was not referring to the warm, smoky stench in the mess-deck below.

"Watch it, Sullivan!" barked CPO Drake, with not a hair out of place, as if the wind did not dare touch a chief petty officer. "I've got my eagle eye on you, laddie."

"All right," Guy said with forced cheerfulness, "let's begin. On the count of three I want you to stretch up —" But he never finished. A cool, crisp voice which could be clearly heard above the howl of the wind, cut in with, "You, that officer in charge of the PT party!"

To his right, CPO Drake saluted in double-quick time as Guy de Gray spun round to face a tall, elegant officer whose blue eyes were as cold as an arctic sky. It was 'Jimmy the One', the ship's second-in-command. Guy had met him only once when he had first come aboard *Ark Royal,* but he knew from the other young subs in the wardroom that the man was a real tartar. "You, CPO, take over the party," Number One rasped, "and get them below out of this freezing cold. You, Lieutenant, follow me. The Captain wants to speak to you."

Five minutes later he was facing the 'Presence' himself, leaning with his elbows askew on the bridge, while all about him was silence and patient industry, with officers and men performing their duties like automatons. The Captain was very tall — afterwards while Guy was still in shock he would have sworn that the man was at least seven feet tall. He was dressed to perfection in a spotless grey duffel-coat with a faultless white silk scarf at his neck, his cap a virginal white, the gold braid looking new and sparkling. He looked at the hapless Guy for what seemed an age before saying, in a cold, precise voice, "Bad form in this weather, de Gray." There was no hesitation about the words, they were a simple statement of fact, like Moses handing down the tablets.

"Yes ... er ... sir. Why?" Guy heard himself utter foolishly, while an attentive Number One looked aghast at him. Had this young upstart gone off his rocker in questioning that august person, God disguised as a senior Captain in the Royal Navy?

The Captain looked at the blushing young officer gravely. "Why?" he echoed. "I shall tell you. Because it's wrong on two counts." He ticked them off on the fingers of a hand clad in a hand-made glove of leather of the finest quality. "One, they are young men going to sea for the first time in their lives. They have to be excused certain failings, Lieutenant." He paused, looking at Guy sternly. "Two, sooner or later they will be going into action against the German enemy." (Later, when Guy had recovered, he told himself that the Captain would be one to use phrases like 'the German enemy'.)

The Captain continued, "They will perform well, like British sailors should do, PT or not. In short, we must not make their lives on board ship more of a burden than it already is. For we do not know how much time they have left." He looked sombrely at the young officer, as Number One strode up to the Captain and whispered urgently into his ear. "Plans, sir ... at once!"

Without turning, the Captain nodded his understanding and said, "All right, de Gray, you may cut along now."

Gray needed no urging. He saluted hastily, did the best about-turn he had ever done in his short naval career and marched smartly away, preventing himself from running by sheer will-power.

The Captain watched him go. Finally, he turned and stalked to where the second-in-command was waiting for him.

Chapter Seven

'Old ABC', as he had been nicknamed by everyone serving in the Med, looked through the window at the ramparts. The initials 'ABC' distinguished him from his brother, who was in charge of the Desert Air Force in North Africa. In the weak autumn sunshine the Barbary apes in their den high up on the Rock were being fed by a spick-and-span Marine corporal, his big ammo-boots gleaming like polished coal.

The white-haired Admiral was not a superstitious man like most sailors, but he did believe the old tradition that as long as the apes, or monkeys or whatever they were, continued to inhabit Gibraltar, British rule there was secure. Even Churchill subscribed to this legend, especially in wartime. He had signalled to the Governor to make special provision for them, hence the Marine corporal with his basket of overripe bananas, brought over specially for the apes from their native Africa. Just how those apes got bananas was a total mystery to Old ABC, he hadn't seen one for years.

Old ABC frowned as he stared at the snow-capped Atlas mountains on the African side of the Med. They were in Franco's hands and the little Spanish dictator would do anything to help his German allies — save go to war with Britain. The unpleasant thought reminded him yet again of the fact that once the carrier appeared in these waters Franco would inform the Germans and then there'd be all hell to pay sooner or later. His frown deepened as he thought more deeply. Franco had his heart in the right place, he had to admit that. He *had* kicked the Reds out of Spain, but during the Civil War there had been some unpleasant brushes between his navy and the Royal Navy. Besides, the greasy little Spanish *Caudillo,* as he styled himself grandly, did look like some hook-nosed Levantine purveyor of dirty postcards.

The Admiral considered for a moment or two while the Marines drilled outside, the gunnery sergeant barking at the immaculate sea-soldiers, his voice full of acid contempt, *"Swing them friggin' arms! Bags of swank now ... Remember who you are ... Open them legs ... If anything falls out, don't worry ... good old Sarg will pick 'em up and post 'em back to yer better 'alf."*

From the most recent signal from *Ark Royal* it looked likely that the ship would make it to the safety of Gibraltar's harbour. The weather in the Bay of Biscay was lousy — as usual — and all German *Luftwaffe* units in the south-west of France had been grounded; and Old ABC doubted whether the Italians would ever attempt to bomb Gib again after their disastrous raid the previous year, when they were aided by the planes of Vichy France. The 'Wops' had no heart for that kind of thing, their style was to launch poison gas from the air onto primitive tribesmen, as they had done in Africa a few years before. No, the *Ark Royal* would be safe in Gib. It was what would happen later when she sailed deeper into the Mediterranean that worried him. What would happen then would be damned nip-and-tuck and he'd hate to face Winnie if he lost Britain's only modern carrier.

"Sir," an educated, refined voice cut into his reverie.

The Admiral turned quickly for such an elderly man, his craggy face revealing none of his worries. There were no bad troops, he always maintained as Napoleon had done, only bad officers. Commanders should always appear as if the sun shone from their arse-holes, he would say, using the crude language of the time when he was a dashing destroyer skipper. "Yes?"

"They're ready for you in the Ops Room, sir," the elegant flag-lieutenant in his spotless dress whites, complete with sword, replied. "Oh, and sir, signal from the *Ark Royal.* She'll be rounding Cape St Vincent soon. All running true to course, no outstanding problems."

"Excellent," Old ABC replied. "Come on, then." He took the flag-lieutenant's arm, as if he were some favourite nephew. They sauntered out of the big, airy, sun-filled room together as if neither had a care in the world.

All his junior admirals and captains were already assembled in the big room, sipping pink gin and talking about the war. They stiffened as the C-in-C Mediterranean entered, but Old ABC did not stand on ceremony, he never had. Instead, he said, “Take your drinks to the table, gentlemen. I don’t want mess-stewards nosing around and listening, so you’ll have to replenish your own glasses from the pitchers on the table. Now, let’s be seated and get on with it. We’ve got a lot of work to get through this afternoon.”

He gave them a minute to settle down, then there was silence broken only by the steady tread of the Marine sentry’s boots on the gravelled walk outside. This was a top-secret meeting, one that might decide the future of the British Imperial forces in the whole theatre. Old ABC cleared his throat and said one word only: “Malta.”

They needed to know no more and understood its significance at once. The conference was going to be on that beleaguered island and what the Royal Navy could do to help.

“It is clear that I do not need to belabour the point,” ABC continued, “that the island cannot last out much longer if it does not get supplies very soon. Not only is food for both military and civilian populations terribly short, but they are running out of ack-ack ammo and — above all — fighters for aerial defence. Once air-cover is knocked out the Huns and Wops can do just what they like with the place. It will be totally defenceless.” He paused to let his words sink in, while they stared straight ahead wrapped in a cocoon of their own thoughts; and from the expressions on their faces those thoughts were not happy ones.

“Now, as usual, Winnie has an idea.” Then hastily he added before they could groan — the Prime Minister was always suggesting impossible ideas that would cost the earth in lives and material to carry out — “This time, however, gentlemen, it is feasible and, on the whole, not a bad one.” He raised his voice, “Obviously, once the *Ark Royal* makes an appearance here in Gib, the Hun is going to figure we are going to make an attempt to run a supply convoy into Malta — and he will be right.”

Again he paused and his listeners waited, they suspected he had not summoned them here from all parts of the Mediterranean to tell them the usual bad news that yet another convoy was going to be run into Malta, with the usual anticipated grievous losses. There had to be something different this time, something that offered a glimpse of hope for the convoy that would soon set out from Gib on that suicidal mission to the Crusaders' island.

"The Wops!" Old ABC surprised them with those two words. "We'll strike the Italian Navy and — hopefully — also one of their convoys to Africa, while our convoy group is still on its way to Malta."

There was an excited burst of comment at that announcement, though much of its content was puzzled question and counter-question. Most of the officers present did not rate the Italian fighting spirit very high. They knew, too, that although the Italian Navy was very modern it lacked modern equipment such as radar and submarine-locating devices. It was the Germans who were the real problem.

Old ABC seemed able to read their minds, for he said, "Why the Wops first?" He answered his own question, "I'll tell you. If the Italians get into trouble, the Hun will have to bail them out as he has done ever since Italy entered the war last year. After all, that's the reason why Rommel's *Afrika Korps* is in North Africa instead of in Russia, where Hitler needs every tank he can get for the drive to Moscow."

He strode over to the big map of the Mediterranean which covered one wall and his gnarled hand, covered with liver spots, swept across it. "The Eastern Basin," he said, "where, God willing, we're going to turn the tables on the Eyeties. We have word from radio intelligence and our spies that the Eyeties are preparing to send a large convoy of reinforcement and supplies to North Africa, Tripoli probably, within the next seven days.

"We've already had some considerable success against the Wops in the Eastern Basin area. As you know, last week our sub HMS *Upholder* sunk two Hun troopships there, both 19,000-tonners and packed with troops for Rommel's *Afrika Korps.* Despite that, the Eyeties are going to go one bigger and send a full-scale convoy from somewhere in the toe of Italy and we shall be waiting for them, here, off Cape Spartivento. There, we shall destroy the Wop ships, lock, stock and barrel!"

"But with what, sir?" came the question, a little petulantly.

"Force K," said Old ABC.

"Force K?"

"Yes, as secretly as possible" — and he smiled at the questioner — "and it appears from your question, Captain, that that secret has been well kept. We have built up a striking force of two 6-in cruisers, HMS *Aurora* and *Penelope,* and two destroyers in Malta, all commanded by Captain G W Agnew in *Aurora.* That force has been named 'Force K'."

He waited until the excited buzz died down before continuing. "So, once we know that the *Ark Royal* force, commanded from the battlecruiser *Nelson,* is under way — and it will be scheduled to sail with the Malta relief supplies at the same time as the Wops leave port for Africa, then Captain Agnew's Force K will go into action. They have been a great success so far in intercepting Italian convoys to Tripoli."

"But, sir," the same officer as before objected, "how will Captain Agnew know *exactly* where the Wop convoy will be?"

Old ABC gave the man his craggy smile, full of confidence and based on nearly half a century at sea. "Because we've been working on the problem ever since Winnie gave the order to relieve Malta." He turned again to the map. "The Eyeties will sail through the Straits of Messina, head for the west coast of Greece — about here — and then push out into the Med bound for Benghazi or Tripoli. Why do we think this is the route they will take? I shall tell you.

"There are three main reasons for them to use this route," he said, ticking them off. "One, by using this route, the Wops will have air-cover for a considerable part of their voyage and two, at the same time, they'll be out of reach of our planes at Malta. Thirdly, although Benghazi is closer to Rommel's front-line, it has been badly damaged by our shelling and bombing, so Tripoli is still the main supply port for the Axis in Libya."

He let the information sink in. "Now, the Eyeties reckon they need a whole squadron of cruisers in order to protect each of their African convoys, plus the normal small craft. The result? Each convoy is a major operation for the Wop Navy. So what will the Germans be forced to do if such a large force of their ally's naval and civilian vessels comes under attack by the Royal Navy?" He beamed at them like a satisfied teacher, happy with the progress of his pupils, whom due to his expert tuition he knew were beginning to give the right answers.

"Break off any action against the convoy from Gib in order to protect the Eyeties. Withdraw their U-boats in the Western Med in the hope they'll find equally fat targets among Agnew's Force K ..."

He had time to flash a glance outside. The ape was still reluctant to accept the banana from the worried Marine. Old ABC frowned but dismissed the sight. This business with the apes and Gib was only a legend, surely?

"So, gentlemen," he concluded, looking directly at Admiral Sir James Somerville, who would command the Malta rescue convoy from his flagship HMS *Nelson,* "if God is on our side, then I believe we shall succeed. Malta will be saved and the Germans will be decoyed into a trap." He indicated the pitchers at intervals along the oaken table. "In the absence of mess stewards, I suggest we help ourselves to some of that pink gin and then drink a proper sailors' toast!"

Quickly, the assembled Navy brass did as ordered. Old ABC was a stickler for tradition and they knew it. They charged their glasses ready to toast whatever the old C-in-C wanted toasting. He brought up his pink gin, hand rock-steady and voice as firm as those long ago days when he bellowed his orders from the open bridge of a First World War destroyer: "To the success of both operations and the downfall of our enemies!" he snapped, *"Success and perdition!"*

"Success and perdition!" they cried as one, their well-fed faces flushed suddenly with the energy and enthusiasm of youth.

Chapter Eight

The mist still hung grey and opaque over the motionless sea, already tinged a blood-red by the great orange ball of the sun rising in the east, somewhere beyond the grey-white blanket.

Seeming to swim in the grey mist, the small Spanish fishing fleet drifted noiselessly. Their heavy carbide lanterns, which attracted the shoals of fish at night, had been extinguished. Aboard the boats the weary fishermen drank the last of their cold coffee and ate the stale *bocadillos* left over from the night before. They hoped they might make a last surprise catch before the fish market opened and earn a few more *pesetas* to help feed their rationed and hungry families. Since General Franco had come to power in Spain two years before, life had been very hard for most fishermen, whom Franco suspected had sided with the hated *rojos,* the Reds. Oil was severely rationed so that they could not venture out far into the bays of the Costa de la Luz and the price of fish was strictly controlled by the Falange authorities.

So it was that Gustavo, bare-foot, ragged and tanned to the colour of old oak, allowed his battered *Marie-Carmen,* engine turned off to save fuel, to drift across the surface of the sea, any sound he might make deadened by the low-lying mist.

Without too much enthusiasm he trawled the *Cabo de Trafalgar,* where he knew there had long ago been a great sea fight. He didn't know exactly who it was between but he suspected that it might have been between the *Christianos* and the *Moros,* who had invaded Spain before the Romans. His teacher had told them about it at the *Escuela des Ninos,* but he had never learned how to read, fishermen did not need such fancy knowledge. But the sea was devoid of fish and he could see from the movements of his friend Pepe that he had found nothing also. It was about then that Gustavo decided it was time to bring his net up and get back to the fish-market with his pathetic catch of *gambas* and *merluza.* He might get lucky and be first home.

But then he heard the sound beyond the mist, a muffled throbbing. He peered into the white fog but could see nothing, but it was there all right, and it was something big. There was no mistaking the thud-thud of very powerful engines, necessary to propel a large ship along. But why risk such a big, powerful craft in these shallow, sometimes treacherous waters? No local skipper, even of a coastal freighter, would do it, it was far too risky.

Then the first big wave came sweeping out of the mist. The mirror-like calmness of the sea's surface was ruffled angrily at the disturbance. *Marie-Carmen* began to rock back and forth and Gustavo snarled *"Hombre!"* and crossed himself.

Then he saw it, a massive, grey shape, threatening and dangerous, towering as high as the church tower at Chipiona. Afraid as he was by this sudden apparition looming high above him, its bow wave advancing frighteningly towards the *Marie-Carmen,* he was intrigued. It was a warship all right, then he glimpsed a limp, white-and-red flag at the ship's stern. "English!" he said aloud in the fashion of lonely men who spend a good deal of time by themselves. "So that's it!"

Then, as it seemed as if the great ship would run him down, he switched on his engine and was chugging out of harm's way as fast as possible, as if the devil-of-the-sea himself was after him. But even in this moment of almost total panic, the unshaven, bare-foot fisherman, with four days' beard on his sun-baked face, took note of the ship's name for future reference. After all, such knowledge often brought money from those quiet gentlemen in the back-streets of Cadiz. The name he noted was *Ark Royal.*

Following his ears, Gustavo trotted along the rough pavement, his eyes lowered every time he spotted the fat-bellied Guardia Civil, automatic rifles slung over their shoulders. He stopped at the sound of castanets, softly clapping hands, the pounding of feet on tiled floors, the muffled cry of the *gitanos.* He did not like gypsies, in fact he felt superior to them. They were little better than the *Moros* anyway, but that German liked the *cantenas* and if he was anywhere, even at this time of the morning, he'd be there with the rest of the local *flamenqueros,* good-for-nothings who had plenty of money and did not have to work all night like poor fishermen.

Still, they said *'El Aleman'* paid well for information and that was all that concerned Gustavo. The German was well in with the Guardia too, and he might well earn a decent sum this fine September morning — so long as he gave them a little *propina,* a tip.

Even now, the shabby little *cantina* was packed, heavy with sex, smoke and the stink of tripe in garlic sauce. The German was there too, dressed like one of the *flamenqueros,* but the pin-striped suit was too tight for him and he was sweating in the heat. One of the gipsy women, who would be dancing soon, was all smiles and come-hither glances as if the plump German was an answer to all her prayers, but he could see that she was doing it strictly for the money she could wheedle out of him once she had danced and got him all worked up.

Gustavo hesitantly pushed himself to the bar, knowing that he didn't really belong in a place like this, even the *Moros* were staring at him. Embarrassed, he ordered a small cognac and then approached the German.

For a few moments it seemed that the German, who at least spoke Castilian, didn't understand his dialect, which was more like the language of Portugal, just up the coast. But when Gustavo said *'Ark Royal'* the German forgot everything, even that simpering *moro's* big, bulging breasts, and suddenly seemed to understand everything that was said.

Hurriedly, he pushed the bare-foot fisherman outside into the shade, not even allowing him to finish his cognac. Carefully, as if it were very important, while fingering a bundle of greasy 100-peseta notes, he made Gustavo repeat his story again, saying, "You actually saw the name *Ark Royal?* You are quite certain of that?"

Eagerly, his dark eyes fixed on the money, Gustavo nodded. He was as sure of it as he was of his father's name. In fact, that was not much of an assurance, for in the local tradition his father had gone to work the cod banks off Newfoundland and, once he had discovered he had got Gustavo's mother pregnant, he had never been seen again.

"One more thing," the German asked finally, as if he already knew something of the background to the fisherman's story, and was making one last check to confirm it, "Which way was this great ship sailing?"

Gustavo did not hesitate. "South-east," he answered promptly, "in the direction of Punta Paloma."

"And then Gibraltar?"

Gustavo shrugged. He knew he had the money now. Why should he put himself out further for a foreigner who consorted with those shits of *gitanos?*

"Possibly, senor."

"Himmelherrje!" the German exclaimed. *"Do haben wir esohne Zweifel ..."*

A few moments later a happy Gustavo, richer by a 500-peseta note, more money than he had seen in many a long year, was on his way home, aiming half-hearted kicks at the skinny-ribbed dogs which were foraging lazily in the dirty gutters; and Horst Hartmann, of the German *Abwehr,* the German Secret Service, was running frantically to get to his radio.

Admiral Doenitz, at his HQ in the naval barracks at Murwik, 1200 miles away, and close to the one-time Danish border with the Reich, clapped his skinny hands together in the manner of a delighted schoolboy. The senior signals officer had just read to him Hartmann's message from Spain, which had come via the *Abwehr's* listening station just outside Hamburg.

Already, Doenitz's brain was racing like mad as he worked out the details of what had to be done. Indeed, he had already made his decisions before the officer had completed reading the vital signal. All the commander of the U-Boat Weapon needed to know was the current position of the *Ark Royal.* In due course, the *Abwehr* spies would find out what the Tommy carrier's duties were to be once she sailed from the Rock. With hundreds of Spanish workers employed in Gibraltar, passing back and forth between Gib and La

Linea every morning and night, there was little the Tommies could do to keep secrets from them.

Doenitz waited until he had signed for the signal and the man had departed. Then he called together the key members of his staff and told them his decision.

"Meine Herren," he said, his lean, bitter face revealing nothing save perhaps hate for the British who in the First World War had sunk his ship and imprisoned him. "I am not going to allow the *Ark Royal* to get loose in the Mediterranean, whatever her mission is, and we must assume that she has one. Why else would that drunken sot Churchill risk his most modern aircraft carrier in an inland sea, dominated by ourselves — and, er, the Italians?" He added the last phrase hastily, noting the Italian Navy's representatives at the edge of the group of excited officers.

"No, gentlemen, my U-boats will strike as soon as the *Ark Royal* leaves the safety of the area round Gibraltar." He smiled, "Just 20 miles into the Med and we will sink her without mercy. That will be the end of that damned ship and the 'Poison Dwarf' can have a field-day with his propaganda *apparat."*

It was obvious that his most senior officers were not convinced. "But how will we know, *Herr Admiral,"* asked one, Admiral Godt, "when she does sail? I know we have watchers round the coast of Spain and spies within the Tommies' base itself, but they won't be able to give us an exact time for her sailing. Naturally, the Tommy authorities will ensure that the carrier will leave port at night, when our spies will have left Gibraltar with the rest of the Spanish contract workers, and our coast watcher will not be effective."

There was a murmur of agreement from the other officers present.

But Doenitz's mood of triumph was not shaken. "You are forgetting the Duke," he reminded Godt sternly and flashed the dark, heavily pomaded Italian captain a quick glance. The latter beamed, showing a mouthful of gleaming white teeth, of which he seemed to have too many, glad that the *tedesclzi* were taking his service seriously for once.

Godt nodded. Now he remembered. The Italian naval officer, who had been hiding off Gibraltar for over a month now while spotting Allied shipping wasn't really a duke, but a mere count. But as it appeared to the Germans, the only Italians who seemed to fight as bravely as their compatriots had done against the Germans in the First World War were of the high aristocracy, so he had been elevated to the title of 'Duke'.

"The Duke is hidden within 500 metres of the port of Gibraltar. I know that his hiding place is very vulnerable, a routine Tommy patrol would quickly find him. *Lass uns den Teufel an die Wand nicht malen,"* he added, meaning that problems should not be found before they are there. "However, if his luck holds he'll be able to inform us when the *Ark Royal* sails, and when she does our U-boats will be waiting for her — here." He put his finger on the stretch of water between Spain and the boot of Italy.

A captain cursed. Another said, "That's impossible," and Godt exclaimed, aghast, "But, *Herr Admiral,* you are putting all your eggs in one basket. If those U-boats in such a forward position are unable to locate and sink the Britisher she can range at will in the Med, protected by her own aircraft and her escort vessels."

Doenitz shrugged his narrow shoulders carelessly, as if he could see no problems. "1 have the utmost confidence in my young U-boat skippers. They'll sink the *Ark Royal."* His voice grew louder and full of authority — his sailors loved him, but not his staff officers. They lived in fear and trembling that the lean, bitter-faced admiral might fire them at the drop of a hat.

Doenitz wasted no more time. "All right, gentlemen. There is a lot to be done over the next 24 hours — or 48 — for the British are a slow people. It's that tea they drink, I suppose. But at all events, I want the new crews to be in their boats and at sea, heading westwards to Gibraltar within the next 48 hours."

He looked around him and there was a look of almost naked power and ruthlessness on his face that made some of his officers shiver. *"Meine Herren,"* he said with an air of finality, "by this time next week I want the *Ark Royal* to be history. Thank you, you are dismissed."

Without the usual hustle and bustle of self-important staff officers who value themselves so highly that they feel they need not hide their light under a bushel, they filed out of the conference-room, each man wrapped in his own thoughts and apprehensions.

But not *Grossadmiral* Karl Doenitz. He had no doubts. After all, he had never had a real doubt in his life. He had made his decision and — naturally — it was the right one. His decisions always were. Finally he sat down and began to draft the all-important signal to the Italian code-named the 'Duke'. The stage was set, the actors were there, the drama could commence ...

Part Three

Death Run

Chapter One

It was Guns who had the temerity to ask the God-like Captain of the *Ark Royal* whether there would be any liberty for the crew in Gibraltar. At first it seemed like his request would be refused outright, but then a wintry smile had appeared slowly on the harshly handsome face and a waiting Guns told himself that the skipper was up to one of his tricks — and it was those tricks that had saved the *Ark* time and time again over the past years of the war.

"Yes," the Captain said thoughtfully, "the new drafts can have two liberties in Gib. But be careful and brief them first before they leave the ship."

"Security, sir?" Guns had ventured to ask.

The Captain had then given him the full benefit of that cold smile. "In a way, I suppose you could call it security. The old hands, our regulars, will keep their mouths shut if they *have* found out anything about our mission. It's in their interest not to put the Hun on our scent."

Guns nodded his agreement and had waited.

"It's different with those youngsters of the draft. You know what these Hostilities Only men are like. Full of vim and vinegar. Love to show off. So, they are briefed that when we leave Gib we're heading south-east into the Med and the local spies can draw their own conclusions easily from that. We're going to French North Africa. Clear?"

"Clear, sir," Guns responded immediately, glad to be let off the hook so quickly.

He was about to salute and get on with it, when the Captain's cold smile had vanished and he said, "And watch that none of them gets Cupid's Measles in Gib. You know the trouble with the ladies of the night there and I want a full crew when we sail again. Clear?"

"Cupid's Measles?" Guy de Gray had asked, puzzled, after the briefing as the men, excited and eager to get ashore, jostled each other to find a place in the liberty-boats, under the keen eyes of the shore patrol which would go with them.

CPO Drake grinned and remembered that time long ago when he was so innocent. It had been in Hull's Nelson Road just after he had finished his boy's service. A grizzled old petty officer had taken him to one of the nearest knocking-shops, picked a whore, asked if she was clean and had then shoved him at her open crotch, his face brick-red with embarrassment at being exposed in front of so many men and women.

The petty officer said, 'Go on, lad! Stick it in. She won't mind, she's had more in it than you've had hot dinners.' Afterwards, when he had 'stuck it in' her, the petty officer then said very seriously, 'Remember the three 'Ws', laddie — 'Whip it in, wipe it, and wave goodbye!' Then the PO went off to get a skinful.

Now, CPO Drake looked at the handsome young sublieutenant standing at the bow of the liberty boat as she set off for the quay at the foot of the Rock and thought back to that time. He said quietly to Guy, "Why, sir, 'Cupid's Measles' is the pox and you won't be very popular with Guns or the skipper if you catch a dose this afternoon."

Guy blushed redly at the very thought and muttered something that was unintelligible to the CPO.

"Mind you," Drake went on easily, "it don't do a bloke any harm to get the dirty water off his chest. There's many a young matelot who's bin killed in action and had never got his leg over. Terrible shame!" He shook his grizzled head. "Can't die a friggin' virgin, can yer!" He grinned at his own humour. "Ain't worth living, sir, is it? To die before you have it up!"

Looking at the old CPO out of the corner of his eye, de Gray wondered if the man was 'pulling his pisser' as the draft would have expressed it in their way. Did Drake know that he had never 'had it', that if things went wrong he'd die a virgin? He decided not to press the point. Instead, he asked, trying to control his blushing, "All the chaps did sign the book to say that they'd taken out a — er — French letter, just in case?"

"Yessir, they did. They're all ready for action, as you might say. I mean," he continued, as the launch drew closer to the jetty and Guy could sense that warm, foreign smell that he could only characterise as 'exotic', "Gib ain't no Alex. Hardly out of the liberty-boat there and the whores is grabbing the old how's-yer-father — and yer money too, naturally."

"Naturally," Guy agreed hastily, as if he knew it all of old, wondering at the same time what he would do if a whore grabbed his 'old how's-yer-father'.

"Now then," Drake raised his voice and addressed the excited sailors. "If you do manage to get it over, and some of yer look as if yer couldn't do that with a £5 note in yer hand in the middle of a knocking-shop filled with naked whores —" but he was interrupted by hoots of derision at this and Bunts said, "That'll be the day — not bloody likely!"

Drake had not finished with them. "Afterwards you take yersen off to one of them prof-i —" he gave up trying the pronounce the Greek word, "anyway, one of them places with the green light outside. There'll be one of them pansy blokes from the RAMC inside and he'll show yer how to pump some purple juice up yer cock so yer won't get pox — and don't let him touch it either, cos you might end up like him with yer pocket filled with jars of Vaseline — if yer follow me meaning ..."

This remark was again followed by laughter and derision as the more experienced sailors began to think of the pleasures awaiting them. But Drake was still not finished. "Remember, if you do catch a packet and haven't been to one of them places, you're on the rattle before yer feet touch the deck. Not only that ..." and he was now serious "... if yer do get pox and it's not treated you'll be pissin' five different ways and it'll be yer own blood, got it?"

That last remark subdued the young sailors. Then the launch nudged its way to a stop along the quay, crowded with dark-skinned pedlars offering "nice dirty postcards ... silk stockings ... lovely grubba ..." and the sailors forgot the dire warnings offered by CPO Drake. Even before the old hand in his immaculate whites had tied up they were springing up on to the jetty, ready for 'grumble and grunt' and whatever other pleasures they could find.

"What'll you do, Chiefie?" Guy asked, hesitant now, wondering if he should try for a little 'grumble and grunt' himself.

Drake grinned. "Well, I'm not gonna chance a dose, sir, that's for sure. Imagine how many men there are to each bint in a place like this! I think I'll have a walk round, see if I can get a cheap pair of nylons for the old woman, and sink a couple of ales. For foreign parts, the ale ain't bad in Gib. Sometimes they even have Watneys." He hesitated, and then added, "By the way, sir, if you fancy something," — he winked knowingly — "that they don't serve on toast in the NAAFI, you might use this card."

He slipped a crumpled card into Guy's hand, who looked down at the card, which was adorned with a drawing of a woman wearing nothing but high heels, with a pair of impossibly large breasts. "It's officers' country of course, but they used to be clean there and the prices aren't too stiff — though everything else is!" and he was about to walk off as Guy said, "Thanks a million, Chiefie. I wouldn't be surprised if I didn't just use your card. Well, I'll be seeing you — and this time, Chiefie, don't salute!"

The old CPO's heart went out to the boy, for that was all he was. At that moment the young officer seemed so vulnerable and Drake wished that there could have been some more satisfactory method of finding a willing whore and perching the lad on top of her for his first — and perhaps his last — fling.

He knew, with absolute certainty, that Guy de Gray did not stand a chance in Hell. He was fated to die young. But there was no way that he could carry out what he thought. What happened during the next few hours lay in the lap of the gods. So he contained himself with a salute, a wink and a whispered, "Don't do anything I wouldn't do, sir!"

Then CPO Drake walked away into the crowds of servicemen looking for excitement and satisfaction in the bustle of Gibraltar's narrow streets, above which the great Rock loomed.

Guy had not realised that Gibraltar was so big. He seemed to have walked for hours, at least his feet felt like it. They were hot and tired as he kept dodging the crowds of tipsy sailors, off-duty soldiers, whom the Navy called 'brown jobs', and civilians of all kinds, dark, small and excitable, who everywhere were trying to sell their wares to the servicemen thronging Main Street.

Guy had not noticed any prostitutes, although some of the older hawkers had their blouses open shamelessly as they suckled swarthy infants at big, swollen, blue-veined breasts. He looked away instantly of course, remembering his mother's comment, "There's nothing more revolting than the sight of a woman thrusting the point of her breast in some wretched child's greedy mouth!"

And while he hadn't seen any whores, he did look at the notices put up everywhere by the Garrison police, warning against the dangers of prostitutes. Invariably, they showed seductive females, with inviting phrases such as *'Do you want it? We've got it!'* coming from their scarlet-painted mouths, but in every case above the head was a hypodermic needle emphasising the grim result of venereal disease. Guy's head automatically turned away from every one of those posters.

Sight-seeing is tiring and he tended to keep looking at his wrist-watch more and more as the light faded and the blood-red ball of the sun was beginning to dip behind Algeciras across the bay. Here and there, naphtha flares created flickering images in the streets, for there was no blackout to speak of.

Soon, he knew from CPO Drake, the Garrison bugler would sound the call at the frontier post barrier, indicating that all Spanish day workers should begin to make their way back to their own country. A foot-sore Guy told himself that he would return to the liberty-boat then, even if he had to wait about until 2100 hours when it sailed back to the *Ark Royal.* But it did not matter, he had seen enough.

At 1900 hours, as the Rock started to come alive for the evening, with the bars beginning to fill up and the various shore patrols, Navy and Army, making themselves obvious at full strength in the dusty streets, Guy turned and stopped at a wayside kiosk to buy himself a glass of cold beer. It was thirst-quenching and weak, probably of Spanish origin, and he told himself that Mummy wouldn't object too much, although she always complained about 'men who drink'. Still, he reminded himself that Mummy and Eastbourne were a long way away and he had to learn how to stand on his own feet at last. After all, he had been entrusted with the lives of 20-odd young men.

It was almost as if that thought summoned up reality in the shape of the two oppos Bunts and Sparks, for they suddenly appeared round the corner, obviously well inebriated and clinging to the arms of a pair of giggling, flashy 'ladies of the night', who to Guy looked old enough to have been their mothers. Not that that would have worried the two matelots at that moment. As Guy turned his face quickly away from them they stumbled by, clutching their whores, with a well-oiled Bunts muttering, "I'm gonna shove it up her, matey, till her friggin' optics pop out of her friggin' frames."

Sparks guffawed and said, "That'll be the day. Anyway, yer'll get yer share of it!" and the Spanish whore with him laughed and whispered something to her companion. Then the four were gone, staggering off to God knows where. Guy grimaced and then sighed at the thought of just how easy it was for a matelot who had no responsibilities.

He turned to head for the liberty-boat, when suddenly a girlish voice that seemed to come from nowhere said, "Is the gentleman sad?"

He turned as if shot, wondering who it was.

A pretty girl, who at first he thought was a child, but then he saw that she had sizeable breasts, was looking up at his face with a pair of large, dark eyes which contrasted with her blonde hair. He knew he was blushing as usual and was glad of the gathering darkness. "Did you say something, miss?" he asked.

She nodded and licked dry lips. The gesture was obvious. "Would you like a lemonade?" he asked slowly and carefully and then she laughed. "Oh! My English is better than that, lieutenant. Yes, I would very much like a lemonade!" Then she flashed a look up and down the street. "And something else — if you wish," lowering her eyes and fluttering her eyelashes.

That reply went through him like a knife. *She was on the game!* What the hell was he going to do? They were still by the small kiosk, so he bought her a glass of the green fizzy liquid and she downed it eagerly like a greedy child. But there was nothing childlike and innocent about her next words.

"I have no bed," she said, gasping as she finished off the glass of lemonade. "But there is a place," she nodded her pretty head towards the alley to the rear of the kiosk. "I know what matelots like. I can give you what you want there, gentleman officer." And again her eyelids fluttered but this time there was something knowing and professionally sexy in her expression and her gesture.

Guy felt his head reeling, his face was hot and his first instinct was to snap an angry reply and stride away. But at the same time he knew that he would never again get such an opportunity to lose his virginity. She had found *him,* he had not looked for a whore.

"I don't —" he began, his breath coming in short gasps, as if he were in pain.

The girl's hand closed on his arm. "Don't say any more," she said, "I will take care of you."

Then Guy jumped back, for he had felt her hand wander down to his crotch and feel him. "No!" he heard himself mutter, "You mustn't!" but there was no conviction in his half-hearted protest. Her fingers sneaked inside his trousers and took hold of the hardness there. "Oh, my God!" he sobbed as she led him like a lamb to the slaughter into that dark alley, her voice low and insidious as she began asking her questions.

Afterwards he had no idea what she had asked, but by the time he had come to terms with the wonderful, perverted things she had done to him and for him, things that he had never imagined in his wildest, innocent dreams, he wondered why she had picked him from all the other sailors in Gibraltar. But it didn't matter, by then he was past any thought.

Chapter Two

Carlo de la Penne, known as the 'Duke', crept carefully down the dark companion-way of the submerged freighter outside Gibraltar, trying to wade through the ankle-deep water while making the least possible noise. It was an hour yet to dawn and outside all was quiet on the Rock, some 200 or 300 metres away. However, the dark, muscular Italian with his long, aristocratic face, was very careful. Everyone, especially the *tedeschi,* thought they were slow and stupid, were all too concerned with their cups of tea.

Ever since Alexandria and that short spell in English captivity, until he had managed a daring escape, he had known differently. The English were a cruel, cunning, devious race; one had to treat them with kid-gloves if one wanted to keep out of trouble.

He waded on, his shadow thrown in grotesque distortion on to the dripping sides of the sunken freighter, listening to the scratching of the rats' claws as they tried to escape. They were everywhere in the darkness and he hated the beasts, but they were one of the things he had to accept in return for the perfect cover the half-submerged, apparently abandoned freighter provided.

De la Penne had found it by chance. After his escape from the English in Alexandria, the *Commando Supremo* in Rome had wanted to keep him under wraps. Indeed, his uncle, the tiny, posturing King of Italy, had asked personally that he should be kept away from the front. But the 'Duke', as he was aware the *tedeschi* called him, had pleaded and begged until they had finally sent him to a quiet sector in Franco's Spain.

Here, his duties had been to spy on the British shipping entering and leaving the Rock. It was an easy task, except that there were times each day, mostly after dark, when he could not carry out those duties. Then one day he had put on his mask and flippers and started to explore the waters off Gibraltar, looking for a safe observation post.

Almost immediately he had found the wreck of the torpedoed freighter, although he had never discovered her nationality, the name plate having long rusted away. But this did not matter, for with a blinding revelation he realised that this was the perfect place from which to watch Allied shipping. The freighter was marked by buoys to keep shipping away from the wreck, which made it an ideal safe place a mere few hundred metres away from Gib.

The *Commando Supremo,* seconded by the coast watchers of the German *Abwehr,* had immediately accepted his brilliant idea. Within days, working through the hours of darkness and using labour brought in from the Italian Navy, a cunningly concealed door had been cut in the freighter's hull below the water-line. Then electricity had been run out by cable along the sea-bed from Spain, followed by necessary supplies including a cooker, so that men could stay hidden in the wreck for days. Within a month of his idea he was in command of the hidden observation post, monitoring the comings and goings of most of the Allied shipping to and from the Rock.

Now, after the tip-off from the poverty-stricken little amateur whore, whom the Duke correctly guessed was the product of some Englishman and a local Spanish woman, he wanted to investigate the carrier a little more closely. Already the demands for information were flooding in from the *Commando Supremo* — and the *Abwehr,* for the *tedeschi* dearly wanted the kudos of sinking the *Ark Royal* for themselves. The Duke frowned at the thought as he came closer to the exit-door to the sea. He was no friend of the Germans. He guessed that after the war, *il Duce,* despite his bombastic boasting, would become the junior partner in Hitler's Axis.

The Duke dismissed the problem as Toni, the exit lookout, rose from the packing-case which acted as his chair, apparently quite unconcerned that he was seated up to his knees in icy sea-water. *"Va bene?"*

"Si, signor Capitano," the tough-looking little petty officer from Sicily, who had escaped with him, replied, *"Tutto calme."*

"Bene," he nodded. Then carefully, even though everything was as he said, calm, Toni started to undo the well-greased screws which held the under-water door in place. He almost completed the task before he slipped his mask on to prepare for whatever water might pour in before he could close the panel again. The Duke did the same and jerked his right fist up and down three times — the Italian infantry signal for action.

Toni acted swiftly. He loosened the last door-screw, pulled the panel open and shoved the Duke through the tight opening; then even as the officer disappeared in a flurry of angry bubbles and the water came rushing in, the petty officer was using all his considerable strength to force the door shut once more.

With his flippers, even though he was swimming underwater, the Duke swiftly covered the distance between the freighter and the harbour. Already he could feel the freezing cold starting to creep into his body, but he kept on and stayed below the surface now he was approaching the danger area.

Searchlights swept the dark area of water to his immediate front and here and there he glimpsed the buoys which supported the anti-submarine nets, those huge curtains of steel wire positioned to protect the hulls of the capital ships at their berths. If he became caught in one of those the Duke knew he would be finished. Even if he didn't drown in his frantic efforts to get free, some alert lookout on the deck of an Allied warship would raise the alarm and a machine-gun would quickly end his life in a burst of tracer.

The Duke dived deeper as he neared the searchlight beams, praying that he wouldn't become entangled in a net. The cold was now really getting into him, he felt that he would not be able to stand it much longer at this depth. He wondered who the idiot was who maintained that the Med was warm at all levels? He forced himself to count to ten, then he began to rise toward the surface, controlling his rate of ascent so that when he reached the surface he would not create a splash and a circle of ripples that would immediately give him away.

Then he broke surface and made a quick survey of his position. The searchlights were between him and the half-sunken freighter and he knew that he had got through the cordon of anti-submarine netting. The Duke trod water until at last he spotted the unmistakeable flat shape of the *Ark Royal.*

He wasted no more time, the trick was to keep moving all the time by swimming slowly, paddling easily or using the breast-stroke, which did not disturb the water as much as his usual crawl would do. Slowly, creating as little disturbance as possible, the Duke swam towards the giant aircraft carrier. As he came closer he could hear the regular throb of machinery, unlike the other capital ships he had passed which had settled down for the night, so why not the *Ark Royal?*

He heard sounds coming from the quay, faint but definitely there; shouted orders, the clatter of a derrick, the revving of vehicle engines, and then he knew the answer. The big carrier was being prepared for her move out to sea.

According to that little whore, the unknown British officer had agreed to meet her again at her pitch 'tomorrow evening'. So it appeared — if he was telling the truth (which men, especially the cunning English, rarely did to whores) — the carrier was not sailing this night, but probably the following one. He trod water and stared upwards at the flight-deck of the *Ark Royal,* having to crane his neck to do so.

But what was the aircraft carrier's destination? That was the all-important, vital question. If he found that secret out he might even get the *Commando Supremo* to move faster than usual and beat the Germans to the attack. How delighted the *Duce* would be if the Italian Navy, and not the German *Kriegsmarine,* managed to sink the great British carrier, the most powerful ship in what Mussolini called *Mare Nostrum* — 'our sea' — which unfortunately had turned out to belong to Germany.

The Duke spat out a mouthful of the evil, oil-scummed sea-water that lay in the harbour and pondered the matter as he trod water. But even as he did so, he knew that his luck could not hold for ever, he had to make his decision and get back safely to the freighter. It was thus, while he was deep in thought, that he heard the rumble of heavier trucks moving down to the quay, where he had seen other vehicles loading onto the *Ark Royal.* The Duke popped his head up, still treading water, and tried to make out what the new arrivals were. Then he saw very long crates which, although they appeared to be heavy, were easily handled by the loading crews and the men on the ship-board derricks. What on earth could they be?

Then — astonishingly — it came to him as he noticed long, thinner crates too, also waiting to be winched on board. It was obvious — they were wings! The *Ark Royal* was loading wings, which would be attached to aircraft fuselages. He bit his bottom lip, tense with excitement at his discovery. The carrier had a full complement of her own aircraft, so why these new planes, which anyway were crated and obviously not intended for the ship's use. Where on earth was the carrier taking them?

Some 50 feet away from the Italian treading water in the sea round *Ark Royal,* and turning restlessly in his bunk, Guy could not sleep. He was hot and bothered, tormented by that 'little girl', as he had thought of her, although he now realised that she was a very depraved young woman. Ever since he had left her and returned to the liberty-boat, where he had received a very strange look from CPO Drake, he had been blushing constantly while remembering the lurid details of what had happened to him down that dark alley.

"Christ Almighty!" he had cursed more than once, even though he knew Mummy would have been horrified, but he had had a beginner's sexual orgy inside of an hour. Indeed, by the time she was coming to the end of her repertoire and he was virtually exhausted, the proceedings had long left the beginner's stage! Guy, panting like a dog in heat, had never realised to how many uses the human hand — and tongue — could be put.

Again, he visualised her as she had knelt down in the alley, which smelled of poverty, animal urine and ancient lechery, and had cupped her hands round his member so tenderly. The things she did with her mouth had made him want to die with pleasure. His whole body was suffused by the unimaginable shock as her tongue began its work, leaving him writhing and clenching his fists and cursing out loud. What delight, what ecstasy! There could not, he told himself, have ever been a moment like that between two people.

That memory of ultimate sexual pleasure was suddenly cut short by a strange slithering sound. Even in the short time he had spent aboard the *Ark Royal* he had come to identify the typical noises of the great vessel, the creak of timber, the steady flow of water beneath the hull, the remote, routine bells. But this was different, a slow, deliberate slithering rather like that of some giant snake — and it was coming from the hull not so many yards away from where he lay in his bunk, tormented beneath the damp, rumpled sheets by the memory of the previous evening.

His erection vanished as he found his whole attention being concentrated on that strange sound. For a moment or two he resisted the need to get up and investigate, fingering himself in the vain hope that he could be transported back to that dark alley off Main Street. But it was not to be.

Pulling on his cap as a symbol of authority he swung out of his bunk, and then as an afterthought grabbed his revolver in its holster, hanging behind the cabin door. Thus attired, he crept through the draft's quarters, past the snores from bodies in the hammocks suspended above the steel mess-table still littered with the debris of the last meal.

The deck outside seemed deserted, though he knew that there were lookouts somewhere about. But for the moment his curiosity was too intense for him to try to locate and alert them. He crept between the massed banks of machine-guns, feeling the coolness of the deck on his bare feet. Suddenly — and he knew the impulse was a foolish one — he felt the need to draw his revolver. He hesitated, but finally he did so as he approached the rails from roughly where the strange sound was coming. Guy craned his neck and peered over the side. For a moment he saw nothing but the dark wash of the water below.

Then he saw it, a black object against the blacker one of the sea. A human form with strange, long flippers was climbing the Jacob's ladder hanging over the side, pausing every few rungs, and Guy, trembling with excitement, knew that the intruder was up to no good. He cleared his throat and cried, *"Who goes there?"*

The old challenge seemed absurd. He could hardly believe that it was himself calling it. On the ladder the figure froze and then Guy sensed rather than saw that, whoever it was, was about to fling himself backwards into the water. He didn't hesitate, and pressed the trigger of his .38. There was a sharp, harsh crack and the man on the ladder screamed horribly, then fell backwards, arms flailing.

And then all hell broke loose aboard *Ark Royal.*

Chapter Three

The flap was over, the great ship had calmed down and the off-duty watch had returned to their mess and hammocks to get a few more hours' sleep before their turn came round. But in the Captain's state-room on the deck above there was activity. Jimmy-the-One had posted double lookouts and Marine sentries, just in case.

In the centre of the large aft-cabin, with its many mementoes of a life-time at sea, the Captain, as remote as ever, listened gravely as Guns and Jimmy-the One discussed the strange events of the night.

In the next cabin was a rigid Marine corporal with rifle and fixed bayonet and a somewhat worried Guy de Gray, still in his pyjamas and feeling absurd with bare feet in the near-presence of those august personalities. They were guarding the intruder, from whom came muffled cries as the Surgeon-Commander doctored his wound without the aid of a pain-killer.

Guy had felt the order rather cruel — at least the man's pain should be eased, he thought. Later, he realised that the Captain had given that unusual order not as a means of punishment but in order to fit into his own devious plan for the wounded man.

Guns had dismissed the intruder's strange gear of goggles and some kind of breathing equipment looking like the escape gear used by submariners, and the great rubber fish-like flippers which had first alerted Guy. "I've heard of these chaps," he said. "They swim up and attach limpet mines and the like to hulls of our ships. They're saboteurs more or less, a typical nasty Wop trick."

"But Guns," Jimmy-the-One objected, "this chap didn't even have a gun with him, never mind a limpet mine. So what do you make of that?"

Guns scratched his cropped, blond head and took a large sip of his pink gin, which all three senior officers were drinking even though it was three o'clock in the morning. "Not much, I suppose, Number One," Guns replied and lapsed into silence.

For what seemed an age a heavy, brooding silence hung over the Captain's state-room, broken only by the steady, heavy-booted tread of the sentries outside and the muted moans of the prisoner in the next cabin. Then the Captain ordered de Gray to join him, even though he was impossibly attired, and the two senior officers.

Suddenly the Captain spoke and caught everyone by surprise. "I know that Eyetie in there, gentlemen," he said. "His name is de la Penne."

Guy shot the Captain a quick, puzzled look, but the Captain's face stayed grave and dignified, revealing nothing.

"How do you mean, sir?" his Number Two prompted, mystified, the glass poised at his lips.

"Last year. I was on the *Valiant* in Alex. He and some other Eyeties tried to blow up our ship and the *Queen Elizabeth.* They came up by the old Ras el Tin lighthouse. In what we found later were called 'pig-boats'." As interested as he was in the Captain's revelations, Guy was put off a little by the latter's strange, staccato manner of speech. It was more than clipped in the naval fashion, it was as if someone had taken an axe to spoken English.

"Fortunately for us we caught the Wop devils before they could do much damage, but they *had* slipped from their — er — pig-boats and planted mines on her. Our chief was a hard chap. He put the Eyetie prisoners, including that de la Penne chap we have here, inside the hull and made them sweat it out. With minutes to spare one of the Eyeties told us where they had attached the mines. We cleared the *Valiant.* The *Queen Elizabeth* was not so lucky. Too late. Took a bad knock. Kept her in dry dock for a goodly while."

The Captain paused, while the others, fascinated, wondered where the Captain's story was leading. But for the moment all he said was, "Two weeks later that de la Penne fellow did a bunk from our guards. Resourceful bugger." And for some reason he looked significantly at Guy.

The other two senior officers acknowledged the Captain's statement politely with a nod, but they were as obviously puzzled as was Guy, wondering what the skipper was hinting at. In his strange way, the Captain tried to enlighten them.

"Somehow, I don't think that de la Penne intended to do the same job in Gib. Where's his pig-boat, for example? The tools of his trade? He wasn't even armed." He looked hard at them. "So what was he about?" Then answered his own question. "I think he was on a recce!"

"What kind of recce and what for?" Number One asked.

"He was not going to blow us up. No time for that. My guess is that he was trying to find out our destination and pass it on to the Hun. So I think we ought to tell him!"

Awed as he was by the Captain, even Guy gaped open-mouthed at the skipper's words.

The latter allowed himself a cold smile. "Give him enough info to allow the Hun to set up an ambush, have them concentrate their resources at a place where we won't be. And by then we'll be up and away about our lawful business with the Hun wondering where we've gone."

"But, sir?" Guns stuttered.

"Yes, Guns?"

"De la Penne is our prisoner. How is he going to pass on what he knows to the Hun as you suggest?"

The Captain looked at him as if he were some particularly obtuse, grubby schoolboy and Guns shrank visibly.

"Because he's going to escape, isn't he! But before we allow that, gentlemen, I think we must bait our little trap. Guns, be so kind as to pass me that small-scale map of the Med."

Bewildered by it all, the gunnery officer did as he was charged, while Guy stood transfixed. *The skipper was going to let the Eyetie escape!*

The Captain went swiftly to work. He ran his slide-rule across the map, muttering "Cyprus" and made a quick calculation on the note-pad by its side. Then he said "Alex" and made another calculation. Then the door to the next cabin opened and the Surgeon-

Commander came in and pronounced, "Patched him up best I could, sir." He looked fleetingly at the busy Captain. "I expect he was making a bit of a racket — I would have!"

Making his last calculation, the Captain said aloud, so that anyone in the next cabin could not but fail to hear his words, "Western route out. Northern shortest, but most dangerous." It was then that he seemed to remember the open door and the Italian inside the other room. "Close that door sharpest, de Gray. Look lively, lad. Don't want the Wop to know everything ..."

Five minutes later the confused Marine guard had been dismissed, followed a moment after by the MO and the three senior officers, leaving a bewildered de Gray in sole charge of the prisoner in the otherwise empty stateroom.

Stiffly but happily the youthful U-boat skippers and their crews tumbled out of the trucks and staff-cars which had brought them here. It had been a long, tiring journey from Lyon, but the sight that met them made their weary faces light up in anticipation. It was still bright and sunny, although the sun was beginning to set behind the impressive bulk of Mount Etna on Sicily. But it was not the scenery which cheered them up, it was the fat-bosomed 'waitresses' in their short, black aprons lined up in front of the *Offizierskasino,* ready to serve them supper and anything else they might want ...

At the sight, von der Weide whistled sharply through his front teeth. He smoothed back his sleek blond hair, which he had cut and trimmed every night before he went to bed, just to keep it under control. He knew the effect blond men had on these dark-haired southern Italian woman. Next to him, Utz von Uelzen chortled happily. "Get a load of that one over there, feast your greedy optics on all that wood she's got in front of her door!" He wiped his hand across his mouth as if he were suddenly very thirsty, adding, "We are gonna have a lot of fun and games night!"

He thrust a hand up under the short skirt of one of the so-called waitresses, who were the usual whores hired to welcome U-boat crews on such occasions, and muttered, "By God, this spaghetti-eater hasn't even shaved! She was in too much of a hurry to get a good length of prime German salami!"

But the new arrivals were fated not to have their fun and games this particular summer night. Almost as soon as they had entered the cool, discreet surrounds of the Officers' Club, with its little trio playing in the corner and the short-skirted waitresses hurrying back and forth with drinks, waggling their plump behinds provocatively as they walked, a senior captain, splendid in white summer uniform, came in through the door, put a hand on his ceremonial dirk and announced, *"Meine herren, Willkomen!"*

They turned to stare at the newcomer and a lieutenant-commander with his right hand fondling the naked buttocks of a 'waitress' serving him with a gin-fizz groaned. "Shit on shingle! Here come the orders. Haven't they any feelings for us poor weary sailormen?"

The staff-officer in his elegant uniform, looking very martial, save for the fact that he wore pince-nez and looked like a high-school teacher, cleared his throat pompously, giving orders for the 'waitresses' to leave for the moment. "I am afraid there will be no time for the pleasures of the flesh. That will come later, I am sure." He smiled, his thin lips working.

Von der Weide told himself that this senior official looked as if he had never enjoyed the 'pleasures of the flesh' as he put it. All the same, he listened attentively, the whore forgotten. There were always other whores. In the end, all women sold themselves for one thing or another.

"Your predecessors have made their last inspections of the craft you will take over," the white-uniformed officer went on. "The boats are all in top-class condition, ready to sail at a moment's notice. In fact your crews are already beginning to take over and attend to their new duties."

"They'll enjoy *that,"* Utz von Uelzen muttered cynically, holding on to his own giggling waitress as if he were taking her with him. But the officer was not finished. "Therefore, please have a brief meal, change into your sea-going uniforms and report to the docks for duty at 1500 hours. You sail tonight."

This statement was met by excited chatter and mutterings of protest at the rush. "I, for one, say that a 'blue boy' — a U-boat man — needs to get the dirty water off his chest before he sails on a mission!" someone cried. "You're right, Hans-Dieter," another agreed hotly. "Brings a 'blue boy' good luck to get it in now!"

The senior official in his immaculate white uniform raised his hands for silence. *"Einverstanden, meine herren!"* he agreed. "But we have some startling new information from an agent in Gibraltar which makes it imperative that you sail from here as soon as possible. Now, gentlemen, enjoy your meal. Remember, intelligence briefing at 1500 hours." He raised his elegant grey-gloved hand to the shining peak of his cap and saluted them.

"Great Crap on the Christmas Tree!" someone gasped, in wonder at the sight. "The condemned man ate a hearty breakfast! This one is going to be an Ascension Day Commando, if you ask me." The feeling was mutual, it could well be a one-way trip. But no one was asking him.

All of them were now making their decisions, whether they should eat — they would soon be on the salted and dried rations of the submariners — or enjoy the whores now allowed back into the room. Utz von Uelzen, for one, knew what his priority was going to be. "Come on, old house," he said urgently to von der Weide, "grab yourself a handful of beaver and let's get on with the job while we've got a chance!" He pointed to some of the officers who were already beginning to enjoy the food that had been laid out for the U-boat skippers. "Christ, I hope I never get *that* hungry!"

Kurt von der Weide shook his head, his mind now full of this new assignment.

But his friend pursed his lips contemptuously, opened his mouth to speak, then thought better of it and, dragging the giggling girl with him, hurried to the cloakroom. Moments later, von der Weide, slumped in a battered armchair, could see their images reflected in a large mirror on the opposite wall. Utz, trousers round his ankles, was bent over the girl's naked buttocks, jiggling them energetically as he thrust away, his face so red he looked as if he might have a stroke at any moment.

But von der Weide forgot the rutting pair and concentrated on the problems he knew he would soon face.

Chapter Four

Guy de Gray opened his eyes and raised his head. Next moment he wished he hadn't, for something like two red-hot pokers seemed to be boring their way from the back of his skull to his eyes. He let his head fall back on the pillow.

"Oh, God!" he moaned to the blank wall of the strange cabin. Beneath him the deck vibrated and there was the steady throb of the turbines coming from below. However, for the moment the sounds did not interest him, he was more concerned with the mystery of how he had come to be where he was.

He was still puzzling over it when there was a polite tap on the door. "Yes?" he said thickly, forcing his eyes reluctantly open again. The light from the overhead bulb in its steel cage hurt intolerably. Guy blinked and things came slowly into focus.

Peering across the cabin was a worried CPO Drake, working cap tucked neatly beneath his right arm. "Hallo, sir," he whispered as if afraid someone might hear. "Bribed the Surgeon-Lieutenant's pill-pusher so I could get into the sick bay. Ten Woodbines the greedy sod wanted."

Sick bay? So that's where he was, Guy realised, still unable to ascertain what the vibrations meant.

"Yes," Drake continued, "he sez you'll be as right as rain by morning. That dago must have given yer one hell of a whack. You bled like a stuck pig, the pill-pusher nancy-boy sez, beggin' yer pardon, sir."

"The dago ...?" faltered Guy, then suddenly it all came back to him. The object falling on the floor of the Captain's state-room. The soft foot-fall behind him and his attempt to turn. The smell of hair-cream and bilge-water. Raising his arm to protect his head, too late. Then the hard blow and red and silver flashes exploding in front of his eyes, followed by blackness.

"Christ!" he gasped, sitting bolt upright and wincing with the pain in his head. "I let him go!" Any blood left in his youthful cheeks drained quickly away. "The Captain will hang me from the yard-arm for this!"

Then Drake chuckled softly. "Oh, no he won't, sir!" he soothed. "In fact, Guns said you did your best. The dago is supposed to be a very slippery customer altogether. He's done a bunk like this before. No, sir, they've taken it in their stride. Besides, they've got more on their minds now!"

"What do you mean, Chiefie?" Guy asked, feeling more than somewhat relieved at the CPO's words.

"Well, I don't rightly know, sir," a hesitant Drake said. "High-ranking officers are not known for taking lowly petty officers like me into their confidences."

"Nor low-ranking officers either!" muttered Guy.

"But, sir, I *do* know this, we're heading for action — and soon. Everything's battened down and there's extra ammo for the guns everywhere. Anyone on deck has to wear anti-flash gear and we're soon to begin double-watches. So what does that suggest to you, sir?"

Guy looked at Drake. "Trouble — and soon!"

"Exactly, sir. I know we're supposed to meet a convoy and I think I can guess where that convoy's bound for. But so far there's no sign of it. So why are we going hell-for-leather like this — all on our own?" Chiefie's eyes narrowed as he asked the second question, "And why it is that the skipper was not one little bit worried when that dago did a bunk?"

Drake broke off suddenly, for there were footsteps outside in the companionway leading to the sick bay ruled by 'Number Nine', as the MO was called behind his back for prescribing 'No. 9', a laxative, for most disorders that ailed *Ark Royal's* matelots.

"I'd better nip off now, sir, his nibs is about. He's very touchy about his sick bay. And by the way, sir, the lads all send their best!"

"You mean the draft?"

"Yessir, who else?" and with that CPO Drake had sneaked through the door and was gone, leaving Guy with his mind in a turmoil. In spite of his injured head, his eyes suddenly filled with tears. He had presumed that he had made an awful balls-up of things. Now Drake was telling him that the Captain and Guns were not particularly perturbed that he had let the prisoner escape and that the draft, that bunch of hard young working-class men, who he thought had no respect for him at all, had sent their best wishes. It was almost too good to be true. Soon, the august Captain of the *Ark Royal* would be sending *his* best wishes!

Next moment the bespectacled Surgeon-Lieutenant poked his head round the door and said, "Lucky bugger you are, Sub. Real jammy. Don't know how you do it!"

"Do what, sir?"

"Captain sends his compliments, wishes you well, and says you're not to worry about anything!" said the officer with a face showing total disbelief. Then the Surgeon-Lieutenant made his way down the aisle, shaking his head in wonder and muttering, "Some sods are really lucky ... compliments from the Captain ... what bloody next?" Behind him he left Guy, all his pain now vanished, debating with himself whether he should laugh or cry.

Von der Weide wiped spray from the lenses of his sea-glasses. He stared the length of the U-boat U-81 yet again. Beneath him in the engine-room the diesels were pounding away sweetly and steadily. His predecessors had obviously maintained the submarine well. He looked to port and starboard, but there was no sign of the pack that had emerged from the Italian harbour just under an hour ago. He knew why. Every skipper was out for himself although they supposedly worked as a team. In reality they were all out to make a 'kill' for themselves.

He dropped his binoculars down to the chest of his black oilskins and out of the corner of his sharp eyes he watched the lookouts to make sure they were alert and on their toes. They were. Balanced well, with feet apart to counteract the roll of the U-boat in the swell, they swept their assigned sectors of the horizon dutifully, eyes pressed to their binoculars as if their lives depended on it, which in fact they did. He nodded, satisfied.

"Nigger sweat, sir?" It was one of the cooks with a cup of black coffee. "Thought you might like it now, sir."

"Thanks, Schmutje!" he said, calling the cook by his traditional submariners' nickname of 'Dirty one'. But Kurt von der Weide said it without too much enthusiasm, for he did not encourage that kind of comradeship between the skipper and the crew the way most U-boat captains did. Still, the cook meant well and taking the cup he was about to sip at the scalding hot liquid laced with rum, when a look-out shouted urgently, "Aircraft engines — starboard, sir!"

Von der Weide threw the cup's contents overboard and swung his glasses up. Visibility was lousy and in an hour it would be dark, but he concentrated on searching the grey, lowering sky for the first sight of whatever it was.

And there it was, as the look-out had shouted, a dark object lumbering across the sky very slowly, so slowly that von der Weide suspected that it could not belong to the Axis air-forces. Their aircraft were modern, monoplane and fast. That object seemed to him, as he re-focussed to obtain a better view, to be a biplane. But he lost sight of it and his attention was immediately turned to the fact that the U-boat was bobbing up and down sharply in spite of the fact that the Mediterranean was as smooth as a mirror. It meant that he had run too close to the screw-wash of one of the other U-boats of the flotilla.

Hastily, von der Weide bent over the voice-pipe. "Bridge," he called. "Anything on radar-bearing ..." He rapped out the compass point.

A moment later the voice of his Number One, Trees, came back, metallic and strangely distorted over the connection. "Yes, skipper. The rating spotted an unidentified aircraft and a U-boat. One of our comrades, no doubt."

"Thanks," von der Weide said thoughtfully, a dark suspicion which he could not explain growing in his mind. He added, "Take a bearing on the sub. Don't try to establish contact. Keep radio silence. Follow him at a distance. *Klar?"*

"Klar, Herr Leutnant," came back the dutiful reply, though von der Weide sensed the slight bewilderment in his Number One's voice. He was now wondering at the unusual command, as indeed the Captain himself was. Yet an inner voice was adamant that he should do as he had just ordered.

Time passed leadenly as von der Weide's U-boat ploughed through the turbulence caused by the U-boat some 500 metres ahead, and barely visible in the poor light. All the same, von der Weide's mind churned, trying to assemble the jigsaw. The spaghetti-eater who had escaped from the *Ark Royal* had seen the Tommy skipper's maps. They appeared to indicate that the carrier was intending a lone break-out from Gibraltar and not waiting for the convoy obviously being assembled there.

The escaper had had only minutes to check that map, but according to de la Penne the Tommy had considered three routes which could have led to Malta, Cyprus, or Alexandria, all places where the aircraft the *Ark Royal* was carrying were vitally needed. German Intelligence had decided, however, that Malta was the Tommy's most obvious destination. More importantly *die Abwehr* experts had arrived at the conclusion that the Tommy was out to fool them by taking the shortest, yet most obvious route — northwards to the Italian coast and then dodging along it as far as the tip of the 'boot' until the skipper could make the final dash for Malta and safety.

But even as he considered what the *Abwehr's* experts thought was the Tommy's intention, von der Weide could not but admire the Englishman's boldness. It was right in the tradition of the Royal Navy's great Admiral Nelson, but with a safety factor added: the *Ark Royal* had 60-odd aircraft on board which could act as his eyes and ears to warn him of impending danger. Of course, most of them were the antiquated biplane Fairey Swordfish, but they had the range and it was because of that that he — he paused abruptly in his thoughts. He had heard — and felt — an ominous bumping and scraping along the hull and it did not take a crystal ball to know what had caused it. Urgently he called down the voice-pipe, *"Both - dead slow!"*

There was the click of the telegraph repeater and suddenly the submarine was barely moving through the wash of the other craft to his front. Von der Weide did not have to explain, his look-outs were veterans, they knew what was going on. They tensed, faces sharp and staring as they scanned the surface of the choppy water. Somewhere — perhaps only metres away — there were more enemy mines. That was what the lone aircraft had been up to, laying mines to protect the carrier from an attack.

"Schweinerei!" cursed von der Weide, his raised fists clenched. "The cunning bastard!" It had been a ploy that he had not reckoned on.

The U-boat crept forward slowly and the distance between him and the faster craft in front opened up, so it was obvious that the skipper of the leading submarine was not yet aware of the mines. Fervently, von der Weide prayed, like he had not done since he had left his East Prussian *Volkeschule,* that before disaster struck the other U-boat would lead them through what he suspected was a very thin minefield.

Cautiously, the words of the order sticking in his throat, Kurt commanded that the craft should increase speed in order not to be left behind. But even as he spoke, again he heard that terrifying rustling, scraping sound on the hull, the sound of impending death. But he had to dismiss it and concentrate on keeping the leading submarine's wake in view.

Someone came out on to the bridge. It was the frightened *schmutje* again, with another cup of 'nigger sweat'. "Thought it might help, sir," he quavered, ashen-faced.

Von der Weide forced a laugh. "It's easy when you let some other mug do the sweeping for you!" and he indicated the dark smudge of the U-boat to his front. "Minefields are overstated as long as you keep —" but the rest of the sentence was shattered by a blinding flash and a huge explosion. The submarine rocked crazily, water splashing over the conning-tower and knocking the coffee and the mug out of his hand.

They both saw the other U-boat rear out of the water, seeming to pause in mid-air before crashing down, her back broken, evil black smoke pouring out of her twisted conning-tower.

"Oh, God! Christ on a crutch — " the cook began, but von der Weide yelled furiously "Shut up!" as he bent to the voice-pipe to snap, "Both ahead, half speed!"

The submarine started to pick up speed immediately, as von der Weide prayed that the sinking U-boat had triggered off the last mine in the field so that they would get through.

Five minutes later they were nosing their way carefully through the flotsam from the stricken sub, its conning-tower just above the water. Life-jackets, schnapps bottles, a joint of pork, a fat Italian salami, a dead petty officer in his life-jacket bobbing up and down with open, sightless eyes, and one arm upraised as if waiting for a rescuer to give him a hand and drag him to safety.

But it was not the dead who concerned the watchers as the U-boat slid out of the minefield to safe water, it was the handful of survivors, drenched and black with oil, coughing their lungs out and pleading, pleading for help that would not come. "Over here, mate! ... Here, comrade! ... I'm near finished!"

Von der Weide closed his brain to the pathetic calls. He could not stop now. The wave created by the explosion might well sweep back and bring other mines in their direction. He was through, the survivors would have to look out for themselves.

Next to him, the young, tousle-haired cook who had brought the coffee, was beating the rim of the conning-tower and crying, pleading, "Can't we help them, sir ... for sweet Jesus' sake ...!"

In the end, von der Weide had to round on the man. "That's enough! Get below and about your duties!" He turned away without waiting to see if the sobbing rating was obeying him and went to the voice-pipe. He rasped, his voice revealing nothing, not even relief, "Full ahead, both!"

The U-boat surged forward and on the conning-tower the stony-faced watchers did their job. Behind them they left the survivors — *survivors!* — bobbing up and down as their cries for help grew fainter and fainter until they could be heard no more.

Chapter Five

The *Ark Royal's* Swordfish caught the submarine wolf-pack on the surface. After they had realised they had passed through the enemy minefield, most of the U-boat skippers had dived. It was safer that way. As a result they later needed to surface in order to recharge their electric batteries, which powered them while they were running below the surface, and flooded the interior of the submarine with welcome fresh air.

As the submarines ran along the surface on their diesels the crews down below gratefully sucked in great gulps of clean, salty air and those in the galleys took the opportunity to cook the morning 'nigger sweat and giddiup soup' — made from blocks of dehydrated peas, with the petty officers making their usual cautions, "and no friggin' use of yer fart cannons after we submerge again, the boat stinks of methane as it is!"

But that September dawn, the 11th Wolf Pack was not fated to enjoy the fresh air or the weird mix of coffee and soup, because their attackers had pin-pointed the submarines almost as soon as they had broken the surface. The huge, lumbering torpedo-bombers had swooped out of the grey dawn sky and came in at wave-top height, the eyes of the pilots fixed through their bomb-sights on the half-dozen shapes of the wolf pack wallowing in the swell and spread out over a square mile of sea. Almost immediately the Swordfish formation had broken up, each pilot selecting his own target. There was no time for the U-boats to submerge. Their skippers knew that they would be hit before they had reached a few feet below the surface. The only course of action was to fight it out on top and the gunners on deck and the conning-towers accepted this challenge. It was that or surrender.

Von der Weide knew that he was in for trouble. For a moment, however, his brain seemed paralysed, devoid of ideas. He had no alternative but to fight back until he found some way of getting out of the trouble in which they found themselves — it was all too obvious: they had sailed straight into a trap that the English had set for them.

A blinding wall of hissing white tracer rose to meet the attacking torpedo-bombers. The Mk II Swordfish pilot was experienced and weaved from side to side, rising and falling, as the tracer bullets sliced the air all about his slow, nearly obsolete aircraft dating back to 1933.

Suddenly the biplane lurched as it dropped its 1500 lb torpedo. But the pilot had made a fatal mistake in not sheering off to one side or the other. Instead, he held his course, following the bubbling track of the torpedo. This gave von der Weide his chance. "Knock the Tommy out of the sky!" he screamed at the gunners manning the twin 20 mm flak guns mounted on the step just behind the conning-tower bridge.

His gunners needed no urging, it was sheer self-preservation too. They concentrated their fire on the Swordfish and von der Weide saw canvas and metal being ripped from the fuselage and sparks coming from the rounded cowling of the radial engine.

Then there was fire as petrol ignited, greedy flames licking along the body of the plane. But still it came straight into the vortex of killing steel. The shattered forward area was engulfed by the flames and von der Weide saw the body of the pilot slumped over and the observer just behind him, with white, contorted features, struggling to control the doomed Swordfish. Then he, too, was hit and he sank down out of sight and the plane's nose dropped.

Trailing flame and smoke behind it, the plane hit the sea with a great splash and tumbled over. Its petrol tanks exploded in a gout of fierce flame, then there was nothing except a dirty, swirling sea.

But a new danger was threatening. The sea of burning petrol from the downed plane was creeping towards von der Weide's U-boat. At first he didn't notice the danger, his eyes were scanning the skies for the more imminent dangers from that quarter. Having lured the wolf pack into their trap, those lumbering torpedo-bombers were setting out to eliminate the surprise U-boats one by one before they could make their crash dives.

Other Fleet Air Arm aircraft, Fulmars, carrying only flares but armed with eight .303 inch machine-guns, were circling the extreme edge of the pack. Flare after flare floated down slowly on the tiny parachutes to pin-point the U-boats, the 'Christmas trees' as they were called by both sides, illuminating the subs in their eerie white light and turning the grey dawn into daylight.

Von der Weide saw the danger of the flares. Every U-boat in that circle of glowing, incandescent light would be hunted down mercilessly by the squadron of Swordfish torpedo-bombers circling above. Then as he looked up, the enemy biplanes peeled out of formation and began to press home their attacks in the face of the angry flak being hosed up at them.

But the Tommy pilots were veterans, they wouldn't waste their tin-fish. Each pilot would pick his target, come in as low as he dared and release the murderous torpedo only when he was sure of destroying the U-boat he had selected as his victim.

"Sir! ... Fire, sir! ... Port bow ... fire!"

Von der Weide swung round and saw, horrified, that the burning petrol had reached his U-boat. Already, scarlet tongues of flame were licking greedily against the stained hull and the paint was beginning to bubble in obscene blisters.

Higher and higher rose those awful flames; carried and fed by the wind they had reached the superstructure, and soon they would consume the whole submarine like a gigantic, searing blow-torch. Without awaiting the skipper's orders, men were running back and forth carrying fire-fighting equipment handed up from below.

Frantically, the skipper sought a way out of the area of burning sea. He reasoned that with a bit of luck those Swordfish bombers would not waste a torpedo on his U-boat on the assumption that the sub was already doomed. With only one torpedo, the planes would try to notch up as many kills as they could; each pilot would want to have one certain victim. But if he managed to escape the burning sea and also avoid any torpedoes, where could he hole up? The second wave of planes, and there surely would be one, would come looking for survivors.

To his immediate left another submarine was hit and von der Weide recognised it as von Uelzen's boat by the number on its conning-tower. There would be no more fornicating for him, der Weide told himself. What had the reckless young fool always proclaimed as his 'Four-F' creed? 'Find 'em, feel 'em, fuck 'em — and forget 'em!' It was the end of von Uelzen, his U-boat began to go down rapidly by the bow, rocked by explosions as her ammo and torpedoes exploded, leaving a thick cigar of black smoke rising high as a funeral pyre.

Then von der Weide saw it, silhouetted against the light of the sky: a dark smudge of land to port. He had no time to try to identify it, but his service in the coastal waters of the Mediterranean told him that there were many uninhabited islands, others holding small Italian garrisons and often used to intern political prisoners. Whatever it was, it had to be his place of refuge where he could escape from the Tommy massacre.

His mind made up, he bent to the voice-pipe. "Both, full ahead!" he bellowed above the terrible noise as the Swordfish swooped in and out of the curtain of tracer put up by the doomed wolf pack.

"Full ahead?" his second-in-command queried, the fear in his voice making him totally forget the rules of naval courtesy. "Have you gone mad? The wind will fan those flames into an inferno, it'll be the end of us!"

"No, it won't!" von der Weide replied calmly, for once ignoring the insubordination, for he knew he was doing the correct thing. Seen by the Tommy aircraft as a U-boat supposedly terminally in flames and doomed, it would fool the attackers. The Swordfish pilots would not waste precious torpedoes on a sub that was obviously finished.

He snapped, "I gave an order — FULL AHEAD — BOTH!"

The burning U-boat picked up speed immediately. At once the greedy flames rose higher and higher, crackling and spitting, a monster seeing its prey was evading its grasp. Trailing thick smoke and a blow-torch of flame, the U-boat headed for the smudge of land on the horizon. It was going to be a race for time. But with both hands gripping the edge of the conning-tower so tightly that the knuckles bulged white from his tanned flesh, von der Weide willed the boat to make it.

Life went on as usual in the great, echoing marble Naval Command offices at Alexandria. Immaculate, white-gowned native servants in red tarbooshes swept back and forth; by their filing cabinets, young Wrens flirted with older men; dressed in white and complete with sword, surly-looking officers who had lost their ships waited for news of another command. And all the while typewriters and teleprinters clattered and telephones jingled urgently.

For Old ABC, this had not been a normal sun-lit, hot Egyptian autumn morning. Ever since he had risen and bathed he had existed in a strange limbo, as if everything that was happening outside had really nothing to do with him, for his mind had been concentrated totally on events that *might* be happening on the other side of the Med. Now, as he replaced the red scrambler phone and knew that everything had gone to plan, he breathed a sigh of utter relief. At once he became aware of the familiar sights and sounds outside the window; the wog in his dirty striped gown beating the skinny-ribbed donkey; the fat merchants watching keenly from the shade while mechanically spooning down their favourite dish of cold beans from an enamel bowl; great Nubian slave women, their faces covered in ritual scars, plodding through the noisy throng bearing impossibly heavy loads on their heads. Yes, no doubt he was in Alex.

He sat there for a moment, taking in the sights and sounds, thinking. With his approval, the Captain of the *Ark Royal* had taken his impossible task and it had paid off. The German U-boat pack had been completely destroyed. According to Signals Intelligence, German messages were flashing back and forth from Italy to Germany and vice versa, bearing claims and counter-claims, with everyone trying to put the blame for the destruction of the Wolf Pack on someone else.

Now, protected by her aircraft, the *Ark Royal* was steaming in great zigzags unharmed and unhindered by the enemy, waiting for the vital convoy bound for Malta to catch up with her. Again, Old ABC breathed that sigh of relief at the thought. If things had turned out otherwise he might well have been on a plane bound for London, heading for a painful interview with the PM on just how he had lost Britain's most modern aircraft carrier.

He forgot that other dreadful possibility: resignation. Instead he concentrated on what had to be done in the next few hours once the carrier and the convoy had come together. With their U-boats in something of a disarray, to say the least of it — so far five had been reported sunk and one on fire — the surface of the Med would be left to the Italian Navy. Already, Somerville's Force H had been alerted at Malta. Soon the Royal Navy would have to carry out its strike against the Italian convoy heading for Africa With a bit of luck, that would attract other Eyetie surface units to the scene, to be tackled by Somerville's task force. If everything went well, the vital ships would be inside Valetta Harbour, discharging their war-winning cargoes before the enemy — Wop or Hun — were aware of what all the complicated planning had led to.

He paused and watched as a lieutenant-commander, with rather too-long, dark hair, began surreptitiously to stroke the thigh of a young Wren writer, not aware that he was being observed from the C-in-C's office. For a moment, Old ABC thought of picking the phone up and getting one of his staff to give the horny lieutenant-commander a rocket. Then he thought better of it, relaxed and grinned. "Good luck to you, you lucky bastard!" he murmured half aloud, "Wish it were me!"

Grinning, he watched for a few moments longer before the officer decided he was chancing his arm too much, stroked that enticing thigh for one last time, looked at her quizzically and when she nodded to his unspoken question, walked off to pursue whatever duties he had. Then telling himself that the C-in-C Med couldn't play those kind of games — even if he were still capable — he picked up his simple wooden pen and started to draft his final orders: "It is the intention of this command to ensure that Malta is ..."

Outside, totally unaware that the war in the Middle East was about to take a decisive turn for the better, the young men and women went about their routine business — their little trysts, their romances — unaware that one day when they were old and boring, if — of course — they survived, they could boast to anyone prepared to listen, "I remember that day in Alex well. In fact ..."

Chapter Six

Daylight came late for the Mediterranean as the spread-out convoy plodded on doggedly ever eastwards. The yellow sun peered feebly from the grey horizon, as if it had not got the strength to rise further. There was no roar and surge of the waves and the air was devoid of wind. The ships of the convoy might have been the silent ghosts of those that had been sunk years ago and had somehow been raised to the surface. The only sign of life was the spotter aircraft from *Ark Royal* droning round in circles on the lookout for any possible danger. Just now, it seemed to be a time of limbo, a dead time in the middle of total war.

On the gun-platform the off-duty watch hung out their wet dungarees to dry, while other matelots carried out duties for the cooks, peeling potatoes by the tubful. The duty gunners cleaned and oiled the loading and firing mechanisms of their weapons and greased the shells so that they would slide easily into the breeches.

Together with CPO Drake, Guy de Gray wandered through the groups of men, doing their best to look interested and efficient, although in truth they both felt lazy, even bored, the pair of them yawning regularly. Then Chiefie broke the silence between them. "Nerves," he said.

"Nerves?" Guy asked, "Why, Chiefie?"

"Inner tension, waiting for something to happen," the CPO said, rubbing his long jaw and making a sound like sandpaper on wood.

"Do you think something will happen?" Guy asked, talking easily to Drake in a way that would have been alien to him a few days before.

Drake nodded his grizzled head. "Stands to reason, sir," he answered. "Old Jerry is not gonna let us get away with blowing up his submarines like we did yesterday. They bear a grudge, Jerries do!"

Guy grinned. "I think I would too, Chiefie, if I had suffered losses like that —" but he stopped short as from the merchantman to their port came the urgent sound of alarm gongs, followed an instant later by the shrilling of *Ark Royal's* own klaxons.

"Ring that bell and run like hell!" Bunts yelled and dropped his jack-knife into the half-empty tub of peeled potatoes.

"Watch them taties!" Sparks yelled back, then he, too, was hurrying to the guns with the rest of the draft, pulling on their anti-flash gear and helmets as they did so.

CPO Drake hesitated for a moment. "For what we are about to receive," he intoned gravely, "let the good Lord make us truly thankful." Then he was off toward the guns as the German aircraft came zooming in to take their bloody revenge.

One after another the gun-crews commenced firing, swinging their weapons round as the attacking Heinkel 111s came in low ripping off bursts of cannon-fire and dropping their bombs, which exploded in great flurries of boiling white water, before breaking off to streak the length of the convoy and climbing away fast. All was noise, crazy confusion, the acrid stench of burned cordite and the clanging of shell-cases as they tumbled to the deck.

Above the He 111s were the hovering Stukas, ancient, easy meat for modern fighters but still terrifying as they hung there seemingly motionless. Then the leading dive-bomber gave a quick flip-flap of its inverted gull-wings and then one after the other they were diving out of the sky, sirens wailing menacingly, their pilots simply aiming their aircrafts' noses at the carrier as if intent on crashing kamikaze-like straight into her deck.

The gunners fired all out, knowing too well that not only the ship but their own lives depended upon the accuracy of their aim. It would not be the first time that some fatally wounded Stuka pilot had been seized by a suicidal rage in the last moments of his life and had smashed his plane and its bomb-load onto the deck of some unfortunate Allied ship. The enemy *had* to be knocked out of the sky.

A Stuka was hit, it faltered in its dive as if it had flown into a wall. The pilot fought to retain control by stopping his dive and levelling out, flying low over the convoy and trying to escape his fate, but trailing flames from beneath the fuselage.

There was no chance of escape and the gunners simply kept firing on the crippled dive-bomber, which was flying into a steel curtain of tracer. At first it seemed as if the frantic pilot had made it, as if luck was with him. But Drake yelled above the din, "Come on, you four-eyed fuckers! Knock the bastard down — kill him!"

It seemed as if the gun-crews were obeying the screamed order, for every gun directed its fire on to the Stuka. The plane rocked from side to side, buffeted by the exploding ack-ack shells. Then the pilot's luck ran out, for a shell exploded close and the Stuka's prop fell away, its nose dropped and it started its last vertical dive. Guy could see the pilot struggling, clawing to release his canopy and get out but there was no time. With a tremendous splash the Stuka hit the sea and went straight down.

"Pint of wallop for that man!" CPO Drake yelled happily at the draft's first kill. But their triumph was short-lived.

The wing leaders of the German aircraft had realised that the *Ark Royal,* although her main task was to carry planes, had the most fire-power of the convoy. If they could knock her guns out, they reasoned, they could liquidate the merchantmen and the destroyers much more easily. They radioed for a squadron of Ju 88 fighter-bombers, which soon came winging their way in to concentrate on the carrier and behind them were slower aircraft carrying torpedoes. If the first wave could neutralise the carrier's guns, the torpedo-carrying planes might at least cripple the great ship, even if they could not sink her.

"Look out!" Drake yelled. "Plane coming in at Red Zero!" He broke off abruptly as a torpedo splashed into the sea, swerved and headed for the carrier's bow.

Guy's fingernails dug into his palms until it hurt. He willed the torpedo to miss. Because of the way *Ark Royal* was constructed to provide maximum hangar space below for her planes, her armour was not thick enough to withstand a direct torpedo hit. He began to pray fervently.

The German plane that had released the torpedo was hit and it just fell out of the sky, somersaulting over and over as it hit the sea. Then it disintegrated in a ball of scarlet flame, the draft ducking instinctively as bits and pieces of the plane rained down on them.

Still the thin line of white bubbles created by the torpedo came nearer and nearer to the carrier. But the luck of the *Ark Royal,* which had seen her through attack after attack in these last three terrible years, held. Seemingly out of nowhere one of the tankers of the convoy steamed between the carrier and the track of the torpedo, her skipper obviously not aware of the danger.

Then the torpedo struck the large tanker amidships and a huge explosion caused *Ark Royal* to rock violently. Guy saw a gun-crew together with their triple-barrelled Oerlikon tossed high over the side. The tanker, ablaze, reeled as smoke obscured her from the carrier's crew. It was plain that she had suffered a grievous blow. Just above the water-line a great ragged hole had been ripped open in her hull and she lost way quickly.

Another Heinkel was making its run. Then Sparks and Bunts decided that they had to play a more active role than mere loaders for the gun-crew. In their spare time, rummaging among the gun-lockers, they had come across a long-abandoned Parachute and Cable Rocket device. The PAC was fired as if from a mortar, and trailed a long steel wire behind it which was intended to shear off any part of an attacking aircraft it came into contact with.

Now, cursing furiously to themselves at the sight of the badly damaged tanker, they abandoned their posts next to the huge pile of shell-cases and hurried through the smoke to where the somewhat Heath Robinson device was.

"Get back here, you two!" screamed Drake. "There'll be death for you two, abandoning yer post in the face of the enemy! *Come on back, yer great yeller cowards!"*

But the two oppos were not listening. Perhaps they couldn't with the roar of battle all round them. Hurriedly they searched for where they had set up their novel weapon, stumbling over the battle debris littering the deck. Then suddenly, Sparks tripped and fell, cursing. But as he fell his right hand caught the lanyard which fired the PAC. There was a sharp crack, a puff of green smoke, followed by a flash of scarlet. Next moment the rocket was hissing almost straight upwards, the steel wire snaking behind it.

On the gun-platform Guy and CPO Drake gawped upwards, open-mouthed. "As I live and breathe —." the awe-stricken CPO began, but he never finished that sentence. The rocket had crashed straight into the attacking Heinkel directly above them. There was a boom of metal on metal and the observers dropped quickly to the deck as there came a tremendous explosion. Then one wing of the German bomber came fluttering down like a huge metallic leaf, while blackened pieces of the fuselage and landing-gear crashed down on to the deck. Of the rest of the Heinkel there was no sign. The wing splashed into the sea and started to drift aft.

As if they couldn't believe their eyes, the rest of the German aircraft turned to head back for their bases before the Fairey Fulmar fighters could be launched into the air and get among them. "Christ!" muttered Sparks, "did you see that!"

Scornfully, CPO Drake answered for Sparks' oppo. "Yes, we did. Now you're a friggin' hero. After this lot's over I'm going to ask the Captain to give you a friggin' putty medal!" Then his voice rose to a parade-ground bellow as he shouted, "Now get yer friggin thumbs outa yer friggin' bums and get back to yer posts!" As he turned away to face Guy, his wrinkled old face was grinning with pleasure.

Then Guy de Gray knew that all was well with the world — *Chief Petty Officer Duggie Drake had winked!*

High above them at his own battle-station on the bridge, the Captain, as immaculate as ever in his spotless white muffler and off-white duffel-coat, removed his helmet and rubbed the angry red puckering that ran across his forehead from the helmet's lining. Guns waited attentively, for the Captain was a great man for the studied rituals. The skipper obviously thought they gave a certain steadiness and order even in the most frightening and disorderly situation. At all events, the Captain never wanted to appear ruffled. And Guns understood the skipper's motives: a steady skipper meant a steady crew.

Finally the august personality was ready to speak. "Fine show, Guns. Pass on my congratulations to your chaps, even those amateurs of the draft. Very good shooting towards the end with the PAC. Didn't know we still had one aboard. Jolly good!"

"Thank you, sir," Guns replied dutifully. All the same, he was exceedingly pleased. It wasn't often that the skipper dished out praise.

Next to the Captain, Jimmy-the-One commented, "I've asked the chief mess steward to chill a bottle of champs for tonight, sir, if that's all right with you, sir."

It was, and the skipper added, "And we'll splice the mainbrace for the chaps. They deserve their noggin."

The other two officers nodded their agreement. Through the screen of the battle-bridge they could see the matelots dragging and heaving the wreckage of the shot-down enemy plane to the edge of the flight-deck and push it over into the sea with the expended shell-cases.

The sight seemed to remind the Captain of something, for he forgot the crew's rum ration and said very soberly, "Now, of course, the Hun knows all he wants to know about us — the size of the convoy, type of vessels, those damned vulnerable tankers, number and type of escort and, naturally, the fact that we are present," and for a moment he looked angry, glaring at the nearest tanker.

"Dammit!" cursed Number One. "They'll be working out our destination now, if they haven't done so already."

"Yes," the Captain agreed. "I mean, there can only be one conclusion they can come to — Malta! We're sailing to relieve the siege of the island." He paused before adding, "But all is not lost, gentlemen. If Somerville pulls off his part of the business, we don't need to enter Malta and fart around there until the Hun comes."

Number One and Guns looked shocked at the profanity. It was seldom that the Captain used such language. Perhaps it was a sign of his inner tension.

Number One ventured the question, "How do you mean, sir?"

"We're going to attempt something that no one, except a few brown jobs, have done before. We're going to drop the crates containing the aircraft parts by parachute."

There was more astonishment.

The Captain appeared not to notice this and went on, "We shall use the Swordfish. They'll leave the ship, while the rest of the convoy goes on alone — hoping that Somerville has carried out his part of the show so that the convoy doesn't need aerial protection — about 50 miles off Malta. When they do so, we turn and make a dash for Gib before the Hun is aware of what we're about to do. The Swordfish will catch up with us in due course."

He paused and looked hard at the other two officers. "It's all going to be nip-and-tuck, gentlemen, but with a bit of luck we'll pull it off. Now let's go below and have a look at the bubbly!"

Obediently they followed the Captain, but somehow the heart seemed to have gone out of the two officers. Both were thinking that there were too many imponderables. It needed just one link in the chain to break and the scheme would fall apart.

But the Captain did not have any qualms. He seemed as high-spirited as ever, as if there were no problems. As he entered the warm fug of the wardroom, with the champagne already cooling on the sideboard among the ship's polished silver, he said, "Somehow I think the next 24 hours are going to be decisive. Not only for the old *Ark Royal* but for the whole of the Med, chaps. It's going to be a victory. Not one that will show the general public that the end has come in the Med. No," he shook his head firmly, "it will show that there is light at the end of the tunnel."

His face grew sober for a moment, and he muttered, as if almost to himself, "And by God, after defeat upon defeat — France, Norway, Greece and all the rest of it — not only poor old Winnie but the whole British people need something to cheer them up!"

At the curtained door that led to the galley from the wardroom, the chief mess steward cleared his throat noisily.

The Captain got the message. His face brightened and he raised his voice. "Now that's all the sermonising on my part. God, haven't I been spouting! All right, Dickens, let the bubbly flow!"

"Yessir," the steward answered and began fiddling with the foil on the large bottle. Outside, the ship's siren wailed mournfully for some reason. It sounded like the accompaniment to a dirge of death.

Chapter Seven

In the apartment which the Italian garrison commander had provided, *Oberleutnant* von der Weide woke angry and with a heavy head. Next to him in the sagging bed Adriana turned lazily, her naked body warm and a little sweaty. One hand fell from her pretty face and to her side, revealing her full, fleshy nakedness, her great melons of breasts, the soft stomach like a silken pillow.

On any other occasion Kurt von der Weide would have closed his eyes firmly and reached for those luscious breasts to let his imagination run wild before enjoying the Italian girl's peasant charms. His men joked about it, calling it the 'morning stand-to'. But for him this morning, as the tiny island came to life in that slow, lazy manner of a place where nothing much happens, there was no 'morning stand-to'.

He remembered the previous night, when the Italian commandant, a greasy, run-down infantry *capitano* who had more than his share of gleaming white teeth, had translated the radio news from Rome. The man's German was poor but just sufficient when accompanied by plenty of exaggerated gestures to explain to an angry, frustrated von der Weide that the German *Luftwaffe* had suffered a defeat in the Eastern Mediterranean, and that the damned *Ark Royal,* which he had boasted to himself he would sink, had played a role in that defeat.

Adriana stirred and stretched luxuriously. With her eyes still half-closed she stumbled across the floor to urinate in a bucket with a sigh of relief. Then she said, "You want, *taro mio?"*

He kept his temper with difficulty. "No," he said through gritted teeth, "I have work to do."

She stared back at him. "I make you forget your work."

"No," he said, firmly and reached for his trousers.

Frowning, because the extra *lire* would be useful, she cursed, *"Porto de Madonna!"* then lit a cheap cigarette from a crumpled pack on the bedside table and lay back on the bed, staring at the mosquito-stained ceiling.

Five minutes later, dressed in uniform and clean-shaven (though such niceties did not seem to matter much in this remote Italian outpost; even the sloppy commandant had a week's growth of beard), he strode through the warm sunshine, ignoring the fruit pedlars and bare-footed urchins crying *"carem elos!",* and heading for the jetty, where U-81 was moored.

The fore-part of the submarine was blackened and the paint blistered from that dash through the flaming sea, but that did not matter. What was important was the state of the engines and the torpedoes and their tubes.

Already his men, stripped to the waist, their muscular bodies gleaming in the early sun, were hauling parts of the torpedo tubes out through the forward hatch onto the deck, where fitters were trying to hammer them back into shape. Other crewmen were down below working on the water-logged diesels, the thick, throaty coughs and whines telling von der Weide that so far they would not start.

Lieutenant-Engineer Hansen, who had worked himself up through the ranks during his 20 years' service, was busy urging the men to even greater efforts, giving anyone who incurred his displeasure one of his celebrated tongue-lashings.

Hansen was immediately aware of the skipper as he approached, the old hare seemed to have eyes in the back of his head. He swung round, gave von der Weide a rough-and-ready salute — a raw rookie could, and would, have done better — and got down to business. "Sir, we need a frigging good pump, one that doesn't need the electric motors. They are deteriorating fast!"

"Explain," von der Weide rasped, refraining from wasting time by unnecessary questions. Over at the fort, which held the political prisoners and Sicilian Mafia gangsters whom Mussolini had exiled to the remote island, someone was watching the stranded sub through binoculars. Von der Weide, seeing the glint of glass in the morning sun, told himself that it was probably that fat-bellied Italian commandant. The man spent most of his day spying on everyone through his glasses, suspecting them — even his own men — of being up to no good.

Hansen said, "There is still plenty of sea-water round the diesels. Clear that away, give 'em a good rub down with petrol and they'll start all right. You can take my word for it, skipper!"

"I always do, Chief," said von der Weide. But irony was wasted on Hansen. He was a typical product of the Baltic waterfront. From Hamburg upwards they produced men who were laconic and out-spoken to the point of rudeness. "One thing, sir," he said, glaring at a rating who had just dropped a newly cleaned piece of equipment, "that Macaroni in charge," he indicated the whitewashed fort with its seventeenth century cannon poking through the gaps in the walls, "he's got a pump. Do a right treat to clear the water round the diesels and get them cleaned up."

Von der Weide's hope rose. "Why didn't you tell me this before?" he demanded.

"Because I asked the bloke for the pump and the frigger said I couldn't borrow it. Old Musso or somebody in Rome wouldn't like it. Friggin' sabotage if you ask me!" He glared as if it were his skipper's fault. "Can't trust them friggin' Macaronis. But you're a gent, like. His kind. He might listen to you."

Von der Weide's hand dropped significantly to the holster of his pistol and he fingered the leather flap. "He damned well will listen, Hansen. All right, get on with it. I'll go and see the bastard myself — *now!"* He turned and before Hansen could salute he was striding purposefully to the confrontation with the camp commandant.

Half an hour later von der Weide and Hansen had their pump. With the 88 mm gun on U-81's deck pointing significantly at the nearest wall of the Italian fort, the fitters and their mates laboured mightily below to clear the seawater from round the diesels. Waist-deep, they scraped and rubbed the engines, drying them and then applying the necessary wipe-over with petrol. At intervals, Hansen, his face blackened, stopped the work, ordered the men to move back and then ignited the thin coating of petrol. There would be a blue flash and the smell of burnt fuel, leaving the surface of the engine a dull grey as the burning petrol evaporated the moisture. The process was repeated until Hansen was satisfied.

The work was slow and tedious — and somewhat dangerous in the confined space of the engine-room — but von der Weide was impatient. He clattered topside for a breath of fresh air, well aware that Hansen wouldn't miss him. Indeed the latter would be glad the skipper was out of the way and leaving him in command of the engine-room.

The girl Adriana was standing on the quay, pouting in her silly juvenile way and puffing moodily at yet another cigarette, while the breeze from the sea whipped at her flimsy cotton dress, wrapping it round her so that her charms were revealed to all. Von der Weide caught his breath at the sight. "All that meat and no potatoes!" he muttered to himself, using the traditional submariner's phrase. She really did have plenty of meat on her. Worth a sin or two, that one! he thought.

She must have sensed his renewed interest, for she raised her arms as if reaching for the sky, and her tremendous breasts rode up beneath the thin material, outlining her nipples which he had kissed not many hours before. He swallowed hard at the sight and felt the old thickening in his loins. She read his thoughts, "You like?"

He nodded. "I like."

"You want?"

Von der Weide licked his dry lips and looked carefully round him. There was no one in sight save for a few ragged Italian fishermen on the quay, stolidly mending their nets, and, anyway, the Macaronis didn't count.

He nodded. "Yes. Where? I can't be far away, you know."

"No problem," she grinned, again throwing out those magnificent breasts, "I take care of you close by. Come." It was more of a command than a request, but an aroused von der Weide didn't notice that or the particular look in her eyes. Hurriedly he crossed to where she stood waiting. A moment later he was on his way with her like a lamb being led to slaughter.

They stopped at an ancient, rusting rail overlooking the muddy, oily water of the harbour. The young whore looked left and right — afterwards it had seemed an age to von der Weide — and she seemed to let her gaze linger a little longer than necessary.

"Bene!" she exclaimed, apparently satisfied. She turned, put her hand on his crotch and gave a sigh of supposed surprise at what she felt there, then turned and grasped the rusting rail with both hands,

He knew what to do and taking the hem threw up her dress. As he had expected, she was naked underneath and he gave a little gasp of pleasure at the sight. With one greedy hand he grasped the olive-skinned globes of her rump, with the other he fumbled urgently with his flies. "I'm like a policemen with a big truncheon!" he muttered to himself.

"Rapido!" she gasped, as if she were a virgin eager to dispense with her virginity once and for all. And he needed no urging. *"Halt die Orlon steiff!"* he rasped and thrust himself against her body, meaning "Keep your ears stiff!"

The force of his brutal movement caused her to nearly lose her hold on the rail, but she held on and started waggling her buttocks as if in ecstasy, groaning and screaming in pretended sexual abandon as she thrust herself back onto him as if she just could not get enough of it.

He thrust in and out of her savagely. She for her own part was groaning and moaning as if he was really hurting her, but every time he paused she hissed, *"Non! ... taro mio ... tutto!"* But suddenly her moans and groans ended in a great sigh. Her body arched, her spine like a taut bow; strange animal sounds came from deep inside her throat.

Von der Weide was out of control too. His face was purple, but he laboured until with a cry, almost of rage, he achieved satisfaction.

From the harbour there came a thick, asthmatic whine followed by a series of explosive coughs — Hansen was finally attempting to start his cleaned-up diesels. As he recovered his composure, von der Weide heard faintly the curses of the men on the deck of U-81, every man willing the submarine's engines to start up. Finally, while the girl sagged on the rusty rail, all her passion spent, von der Weide listened to his crew's attempts to start the U-boat's engine and fumbled for his money-belt.

All U-boat skippers were given a number of gold coins to be used in an emergency — and this was certainly not one. But she deserved her reward and he had an inner feeling that he would soon be leaving the island for the final attack. If the attack failed he would not need those gold coins; if it succeeded — and he was convinced that it would — then a grateful Doenitz and his Fuehrer would shower him with wealth, as many gold coins as he wanted.

Her dark eyes flashed as she saw the gold coins and she bent and kissed his fingertips as he handed her the first ones while she murmured, *"Grazie ... molto grazie, signor!"* At that moment the U-boat's diesels burst into loud, triumphant life, and the skipper gave the girl the rest of the coins, seeing her eyes flood with tears of gratitude. *"Io,"* she pointed to herself, "remember you ... *Danke!"*

Then for some reason he could not comprehend, with time running out and concerned solely to get back to his U-boat, he saw the girl turn and look challengingly up at the fort. She held up her fistful of coins and gave that primitive Italian gesture of scorn and derision — slapping her right hand against the biceps of her left arm.

Von der Weide grinned as he heard the alarm klaxon on the U-boat sounding urgently, calling him back and he ran down the cobbled jetty, all cares vanished, while the girl watched him go, her face a mixture of sadness and victory.

Up on the ramparts the Commandant, who had seen everything through his binoculars, cursed and lowered them, his face suffused with rage. *"Porto de Madonna!"* he spat, watching the damned *Tedeschi* spring aboard his craft as it began to creep slowly out into the main channel.

"Bestia!" he snarled after von der Weide, gesturing with absolute blind hatred, "I'll kill you!" Hurriedly he stowed his binoculars in their case, his mind made up. He raced from the ramparts and down the fort's ancient stone staircase, running through the gateway to the street and across the little cobbled *piazza,* his mind too full to acknowledge the sloppy salutes of the ragged soldiers and sailors who stood aside for him.

The Commandant knew how to contact the Allies and he should have thought of it before. The others of his evil breed, the *mafiosi,* called him 'il *Americano'* because he had spent many years in America before he had been deported, where he had formed contacts with them and was now one of the *compadres* in Sicily. Somehow, in spite of all the checks, they managed to get messages through illegally. For a few favours they would oblige and pass on the details of the U-boat.

The Germans who had affronted his honour and insulted him, even if it was with that slut of a peasant girl, a *putana,* would have to pay the ultimate price for that. He gave an evil grin as he vanished round the corner, heading for the cheap cafes where the political prisoners drank their midday *grappa* and played cards interminably. The German submarine and its crew would never leave the Mediterranean.

"DIE, GERMAN!" he cried, shaking his fists at the dwindling shape of U-81.

Chapter Eight

"HIT!" the radar-operator exclaimed, peering joyfully at the eerily green-glowing screen. Guns beamed as he too craned his neck to view the effects of the sea battle taking place some 20 miles away in the darkness. "Force H is really giving the Wops hell!" he chortled.

"You can say that again, sir!" the rating agreed. "We really caught the Eyeties with their knickers down this time!" He made a quick calculation, "Seven merchant-ships and escorts were on the screen at the outset of the battle. Looks as if they've lost four merchantmen already. Probably a couple of the escorts too, but it's hard to be sure. They buzz about all over the sea like blue-arsed flies, sir."

Guns' beam increased. "Excellent! All right, keep up the good work. I'll go up top. The Swordfish are about to take off. I must make sure that my gunners are awake and not having a quiet spit-and-draw somewhere!" The radar-operator nodded, but he did not take his eyes off the screen, which showed ships and men fighting for their lives, even now perhaps dying in agony as he watched.

Up top on the flight-deck all was controlled confusion. Ratings in hoods and overalls, illuminated pads in their hands waiting to signal aircraft up from the flight-deck; duty officers busy with their check-pads; mechanics giving a last boost to the aircraft lined up, engines running prior to take-off; dispatch specialists from Marine Combined Operations checking the planes' loads for stability.

Noise drowned out even the sound of the engines, for the Captain was determined to launch his Swordfish within the next 30 minutes and then make his long dash for the safety of Gibraltar. There were too many aircraft lurking about in the inky darkness above them seeking targets of opportunity, and when Somerville's Force H had dealt with the Italian convoy the survivors racing for home might just bump into the *Ark Royal.* And that was something he could do without.

Striding out, avoiding the ratings running about their duties, Guns stopped momentarily at the gun-pads manned by the draft. He spotted de Gray and old CPO Drake peering out over the side at the scarlet flashes of guns stabbing the darkness. "Hello!" he laughed, "Doing a bit of battle-spotting?"

"Yessir," Guy answered with the eager enthusiasm of youth. "The Eyeties are taking a real pasting, sir!"

"And the treacherous bastards deserve it," the senior officer replied as to port a soundless flash momentarily lit up the whole night sky. "I hope old Musso now realises just what kind of a mess he got his people into last year when he marched into France." Guy made no response, he did not think it was up to him to do so. Besides, the first of the Fairey Swordfish was now revving up to full power and Guns wouldn't have heard him anyway.

There was a loud rumble and swish, the flash of wing-lights and then the Swordfish was off the end of the deck, seemingly about to hit the sea, when it began to lift and roar away as the second aircraft followed. "Brave lot of lads," CPO Drake told himself, wondering how they could summon up the kind of courage that was needed to risk one's life every time one took off or landed on *Ark Royal's* heaving flight-deck.

Plane after plane flashed by and took off, each weighed down by the crate containing aircraft parts which was lashed between its fixed undercarriage. Slowly but surely the old biplanes circled over the carrier gaining height while they got into their squadron formation before flying off to deliver their vital cargoes in Malta about 50 miles away.

* * *

In Malta, the civilian populace had already guessed that once again the British were trying to run a convoy through to their hard-pressed island. At night, the population usually vanished into the old and new rabbit-warrens of caves tunnelled into the island's rock formations. Some families, from ancient, black-clad grandmothers to tiny naked babies, lived permanently down in the tunnels in comparative safety, emerging blinking into the unaccustomed bright sunlight to collect food and oil rations before scuttling back down below while it was safe.

But not this night. As the searchlights swept the dark sky with their white beams and the RAF's night-fighters droned round and round overhead seeking enemy intruders, the Maltese rose like ghosts from their tunnels. They stumbled, silent-footed and hardly speaking, as if the slightest whisper might bring death from the sky, as they made their way down to the harbour. Like patient pack-animals they waited there, huddled together for warmth, obeying the commands of the sentries who were everywhere, all trying to penetrate the darkness and spot the first of their rescuers, who they assumed would be coming in from the sea.

But help was not coming from the sea, but from the sky. As green flares shot into the sky to explode above the only air-strip, illuminating the crater-pocked landscape below, the first aircraft engines were heard. They were coming in low and even before they could be seen the waiting crowd began to mutter in English, "Faith, Hope and Charity!"

These were the names of the three Gladiator fighters which had been shot down in the defence of the island and they were remembered by the hard-pressed defenders as their sole protection against the persistent air-attacks.

Then one by one the familiar shapes, this time from *Ark Royal,* began to approach the airfield, throttling back to near stalling speed to release the crates attached to parachutes onto the runway before revving-up and climbing away again. At first, the crowds of civilians, shabby and half-starved, protected by a cordon of troops, did not know how to react, but then the first supply ship steamed majestically into Valetta Harbour, its sirens hooting while a naval band played 'Rule Britannia' on the jetty. It was the signal for the gathered crowds to break into a tremendous cheer, one that went on and on as if it would never stop.

The Prime Minister always objected to being awakened in the early hours — he had only been to bed three hours before — but he did not reveal his annoyance as Old ABC came through on the scrambler phone from Egypt. Sitting up in his new blue 'siren suit', toothless, but with the usual large cigar between his gums and a glass of whisky on the bedside table, he listened carefully to what the old Admiral had to say. "Somerville's *Hood* has been hit," the PM interjected, but apparently he received a soothing assurance, for he said, "Oh, well, we won't have to worry about the Force's flagship if she can make it hack to port under her own steam. Carry on!"

Again Churchill listened without interrupting as Old ABC gave him further details of the convoy that had just run in to the hard-pressed island, his agile, fertile mind already calculating its effect on Rommel's intentions in North Africa. Without the supplies that the Italians were running into Benghazi for the *Afrika Korps* and with Malta still not overrun and straddling his supply routes, the Desert Fox would have to think again before he launched a full-scale offensive against the British 8th Army. This presented the advantage that Cairo had been asking for ever since Rommel had made his appearance in North Africa. The German would be a tough nut to crack, but crack him they would.

"Splendid ... splendid!" Churchill praised the old Admiral as he finished his report. "Pass on my congratulations to all members of the Mediterranean Fleet for a job well done. It goes without saying that the mainbrace will be spliced in due course. Your chaps deserve a spot of Nelson's blood — they've earned it." He beamed at the red phone as if, far away in Alexandria, the Admiral could see him.

Churchill's smile vanished as he tried to think the present naval operation to its logical conclusion. Outside, the first birds had begun to stir and the tall trees lining the road round St James's Park were beginning to shed their autumn leaves.

"The *Ark Royal —*" he began.

Old ABC beat him to it. "Already on her way back to Gib, Prime Minister," he said. "We thought it best not to run the risk of her entering Valetta Harbour. The Hun will no doubt react violently today and start his bombing again."

"Good thinking," the PM agreed while the Admiral waited, then he dipped the unlit end of his cigar into the tumbler of whisky, twirled it round and took a pleasurable puff at the double Corona. There was a moment's silence, disturbed only by the long-range static of the scrambler phone. Outside, London still slept before waking to face another day of war. For a moment or two Churchill allowed his thoughts to wander to the nation which had rejected him before 1939 as a warmonger, but which now totally depended on him for its future. One major wrong decision on his part and the Nazis would win. It would be the end of the British Empire.

That thought jerked him back to the present. "Well, Admiral, let me emphasise one last point. The successful run of the *Ark Royal* for the Rock is paramount. It will leave a bitter taste, after your splendid victory, if the carrier is sunk — and believe me, the Hun will do his utmost to sink her. She is now a prestige object."

"I take your point fully, sir," said the Admiral, "but don't worry, the Royal Navy will get her back to port safely. You have my word on it!"

"Splendid!" Churchill said again, but without much enthusiasm. As he put the phone down he wondered if his old 'black dog' had come back to plague him yet again, or whether he had had a glimpse of the future — that *Ark Royal* would not make it to safety.

"Morning, sir," Number One said, his tone subdued in spite of the fact that they were now only 50 miles or so away from the Rock. It was the weather that had taken a turn for the worse. It seemed more like winter in the North Sea than the Med in autumn. A cold, vicious wind was sweeping across the sea and hurtling spray at the bridge structure above the flight-deck while the *Ark Royal* swayed and shook under the impact of the huge waves which battered her. High up, the lookouts, red-faced and dripping with salt spray, sheltered as best they could, held in place by life-lines. There could be no flying today, the ship was without her eyes and ears.

"Morning, Number One," the Captain answered, as smart and urbane as ever, the fact that he was in charge of Britain's largest aircraft carrier without even a destroyer escort seemingly not worrying him in the least. "What's the latest?"

"I'll give you the good news first, sir," Number One said, playing the same game as the skipper.

"Do, pray," the Captain said, taking one of his special hand-rolled cigarettes out of his silver case and lighting it with his usual coolness.

"The operation last night, sir, was a hundred per cent success. The convoy got into Malta unscathed, every ship. Mr Churchill signalled Old ABC his congratulations and the C-in-C repeated them to us."

"Thank him when you acknowledge, please."

"I will, sir. Our chaps dropped their cargoes just as successfully. However, here's the bad news. The weather has forced them to turn for Africa. They should be landing at one of the 8th Army fields just about now. As soon as the weather clears they'll head for us. If we're in port by then, naturally they'll fly to Gib."

With a nod, the Captain acknowledged the information, but said nothing. It was not particularly good news, though. There were still two to three hours' sailing time to get into Gib and they were without air cover. He puffed at his Bond Street cigarette a little moodily.

"Just a few odds and ends otherwise," Number One added, glancing idly at his rain-spotted notebook as if he wondered whether he should tell the skipper. But the Captain looked at him and saw the indecision. "Go on ... spit it out, Number One!"

"Well, you know what kind of Nervous Nellies those Intelligence Wallahs are, sir."

The Captain nodded in agreement.

"Apparently they've picked up some kind of saloon-bar gossip, one of their *sources,* as they like to call that kind of thing."

"And?"

"They heard a rumour that a Hun sub is still active in these waters. Seems as if we didn't knock them all out after all." He ended with a sigh. “If this bloody storm isn’t bad enough, we might also have to contend with a U-boat between us and Gib.”

The Captain forced a smile, though he had never felt less like smiling. “These things are sent to try us, Number One.” He raised his voice, “Well, hop to it. Finger out of the orifice as they say and get weaving. Tell the crew to lash and make to. When we enter Gib I want the old *Ark* to look as if she’s on a pre-war pleasure cruise, showing the flag and all that kind of thing!”

“Yessir!” Number One answered promptly, animated by the skipper’s infectious optimism. But at the back of his mind a cynical voice whispered, ‘Not *when* we get to Gib, old fruit, but IF!’

Chapter Nine

Ping ... ping ... ping. The sudden sound stabbed into the heavy silence of the U-81 's interior. Everyone stopped what he was doing, each head turned to one side as they listened to that fatal, frightening *ping ... ping ... ping.*

Von der Weide, hollow-eyed and tired from another day of coaxing the battered, blistered U-boat with its tricky diesel engines through the high seas, was first to react.

"Echo-ranging!" he exclaimed in a tense whisper. "Someone's echo-ranging!" Those who heard him knew what the skipper meant. Up on the surface, a ship was bouncing sonar signals against the submarine's hull. If they were loud enough, the unknown operators would already have heard the echo and located the U-81 lurking in the depths.

For what seemed an age, as the crew froze like figures in a wax tableau, everyone listened. As always those ominous pings gave them a sense of loneliness, for up there was a ship that might have already established their position and was about to sink her without mercy, without remorse. Slowly but surely, their ashen faces became lathered with a greasy sheen of wet, sweaty fear.

Von der Weide knew that he had to act. If he did not, the crew's nerve would crack and when it finally came to violent action, as it surely must, they would make mistakes, hesitate about carrying out an order for that fraction of a second too long, run the risk that U-81 would be sunk before she had a chance to fight.

"Stand by forward tubes one to four," he ordered in a hoarse whisper, for the knowledge that the unknown hunter had locked on to them was already compelling the crew to talk in whispers and walk about on tiptoe. The torpedo ratings and their petty officers moved into their firing positions. One by one, in low tones, the reports came back, "One — standing by, sir." ... "Two — standing by, sir ..."

The U-boat's second-in-command appeared at the skipper's side as he crouched, listening, next to the periscope, his mouth open as if he were a village yokel, concentrating on that *ping ... ping ... ping ...*

"Silent running, sir?" he queried in a whisper.

Von der Weide nodded his agreement. "Yes, it's for the best," he said, but still gave all his attention to the sounds, trying to out-think their hunter up there on the surface.

With beads of sweat standing out on his forehead under the loose lock of lank, blond hair, the young officer snapped his orders out. Every piece of machinery that was creating any kind of noise was closed down and in an instant the cooling system which circulated its fresh breeze throughout the submarine and protected the electrical equipment was stilled and immediately the atmosphere in the U-boat began to foul up. The fetid smell of sweat, stale food and human misery seeped through the compartments. Every rating went over to hand control, closing and opening the flaps, the fins, the giant rudder, by the strength of his own muscles. As they worked, the heat became worse and worse and their shirts and shorts were clinging wetly to their bodies.

Von der Weide saw none of this. His whole concentration was focused on that pinging. The blond rating at the hydrophone was beginning to sing out details of their hunter's position: "Bearing red ... 200 metres ... angle of approach red." Every clipped, strained phrase stabbed at the skipper, he knew that the hunter was now close and approaching at a steady pace. Von der Weide gripped hold of the periscope handles, ready for what he knew had to come within seconds.

Then it did.

Click! The submariners tensed, knowing what was about to happen. The explosion of the depth charge would go through three steps: first that click, then the great hollow thud of metal striking metal, as if the hull were being struck by a giant hammer and thirdly the terrifying boom and thunder as the sea came pounding through any crack in the hull the mine had ripped.

Together, the three stages combined in one numbing, horrifying noise. Eardrums hurt in the pressure, plates and mugs fell from their racks, cork chips and paint flakes showered the deck.

Next to von der Weide's head a light bulb suddenly shattered and he ducked as his head was showered by glass splinters. The U-boat shook and trembled like a wet dog shaking itself dry. To the skipper, it was like a car accident that he had been involved in, he thought.

Dazed, he shook his head violently and forced everything back into focus. Everywhere, the shaken, white-faced crew were picking themselves up from the debris on deck, wet from the bilge water that was swilling about their feet.

He had to act and rapped out orders. The U-81 had to be moved as quickly as possible away from the area of the depth-charging and then immediately back to silent-running. It was the only means of putting their hunter or hunters off the scent.

"Both reverse!" he snapped, *"At the double now, goddamn you!"*

It was obvious that Number One was surprised. Why go back into danger? But he knew von der Weide, he was as unyielding as the toughest of the old-style martinets of the Imperial German Navy. He would tolerate no disobedience. The order was given, followed by the hum of the electric motors. From the crew, looks of apprehension were directed at the Captain, then up to the top of the hull, as if they expected depth-charges to come raining down on them again, to send them to their deaths on the sea-bed. But slowly the submarine moved backwards until von der Weide was satisfied.

"Stop both!" he commanded.

The U-boat very slowly drifted to a stop. Then again there was the wait in tense anticipation, each man wrapped in his personal fears. Were they going to get away with it?

But this time there were no pings, only the thunder of powerful engines as the hunter on the surface grew closer and closer. "Holy Mother of God and Jesus!" a rating moaned, his eyes rolling in their sockets, "protect and save us...!"

"Shut that rubbish up!" von der Weide snarled. "God can't see us down here, you yellow idiot!" and the man's prayers faltered away to nothing.

The thunder overhead grew louder. It drowned out every other sound, it was their whole world and there had never been a time without that shattering noise. Von der Weide's mouth opened as if he were preparing to scream and his second-in-command stared at him in wonder. Was the skipper cracking at last?

But the skipper caught himself in time. He closed his mouth and shut the scream off. Instead, although he did not realise it, his hands started to tremble uncontrollably.

The thunder was directly overhead.

Men howled in fear, their sounds lost, their hands pressing against their ears to prevent their eardrums bursting. The pressure of the depth was beginning to tell, as rivets on the hull began bursting and popping out of their sockets. The glass covers of instruments shattered into sharp splinters, hull plates buckled and water began to squirt through tiny holes.

Von der Weide reacted quickly. There was a plan, hasty and improvised, beginning to form in his mind. It was bold — he was virtually delivering himself up to the enemy. Only once before had he ever heard of it succeeding, but it was all he could think of.

So in the midst of the chaotic, panic-stricken scene, he called out clearly, "BOTH — REVERSE!"

Number One looked at him as if he had gone mad, but he did not challenge the order. It was no longer worthwhile, they were finished and death awaited. Obeying the order gave him something to do without thinking of what was coming. He turned and repeated the command and the engines whined into life.

With a hesitant tremble, the U-81, which was about to become one of the most famous submarines in the history of the German U-Boat Weapon, moved. Another depth-charge exploded nearby, rocking the submarine, but she crawled backwards until a now eager von der Weide, his gaze fixed on the shattered controls, called, "Stop both," and then, "Ahead both ... *Beide Maschinen voraus!"*

While the crew gaped at their skipper, unwilling to believe the evidence of their own ears, the submarine began to inch forward in the same direction as their relentless hunter, which mystifyingly had stopped depth-charging.

Von der Weide, his head cocked to one side and listening eagerly to check if his plan was working, let them wait for a few moments. Then he said, "Men of U-81, I think that now we are directly beneath the Tommy carrier, the *Ark Royal!"*

There was an excited buzz of chatter but he stopped it dead, finger to his lips. "Keep it down to a dull roar, will you," he pleaded softly. "Up top, they know we are here, but we don't want to give too much of our presence away. At this speed we can keep up with her, but once she picks up speed and pulls away — we shall torpedo her!"

He forced a weary but triumphant smile. "For the time being, comrades, we are safe. The Tommies know we are here, but they can't do anything about it. If they drop depth-charges they will blow holes in their own hull. Of course, it would sink us, but it would also sink the *Ark Royal."*

Someone laughed and said, "Sink themselves, that's friggin' rich!" Then they were all laughing like crazy men who have just seen death and avoided it —*for a while.*

Guy de Gray had been fast asleep when the first depth-charge had exploded to the rear of the *Ark Royal.* Someone must have sounded General Quarters, but obviously he had been too exhausted to hear. He had been in his mother's sea-front villa at Eastbourne, surrounded by the pathetic souvenirs of her life and the great Chinese vases filled with dried bulrushes, the ones which had always made the kids at school taunt him with "You weren't born as Moses, were you, Gray Minor?"

In his dream, Mummy had been in one of her protective moods, chiding him for his sins, though the language she used had been decidedly unlike her. "Haven't I told you before not to let those little tarts take your thing in their mouths? You don't know whether they've brushed their teeth! God only knows what they might have had in their mouths beforehand!" Her choice of subject had puzzled him greatly. What had she meant? Had she known about such things all along? Did she want to tell him that he had grown up at last?

Then a crude voice crying in this new language which Mummy obviously understood had wakened him rudely with, "Hands off'n yer tools and on with yer socks. Old Jerry's here!"

The whole ship was now alert. The buzz went from division to division as the men struggled into their bad-weather gear and braved the climb to the deck to face the terrible weather.

"There's a friggin' Jerry sub right underneath us. Found it on the radar. And there ain't a friggin' thing the skipper can do about it at the moment ..."

Guy de Gray fought his way along the wet and slippery deck of the *Ark Royal,* hanging onto the life-lines as the terrible wind buffeted him, pulling and pushing at his body and threatening to hurl him over the side and into the heaving, spume-flecked maelstrom all round her.

In spite of the weather, the draft had all turned out, so far as the young officer could see, the water streaming in rivulets down his wind-reddened face. He cupped his hands about his mouth and bellowed, "Close up to the guns!" Obediently, the men did so, clinging to the stanchions and inching along foot by foot until they slumped into their metal seats and began buckling themselves into position. Guy took a quick glance at the mountainous waves, sometimes sweeping right over the flight-deck and scattering pails, brooms and any loose equipment back and forth in heaps.

He could now understand the Captain's dilemma. Up there in the barely visible bridgehouse he was being forced to make his decision. Should the *Ark Royal* continue on with the desperate U-boat sheltered below her, with the German skipper perhaps at the end of his tether and ready to fall in behind the carrier and try to torpedo her before making a run for it? Or should he order top speed and run the risk to his ship by doing so, but hopefully leaving the submarine behind?

Guy frowned hopelessly and wiped the spray from his face with a soaking wet sleeve. He was so glad that he wasn't up there in the Captain's shoes. Not only was there the problem of the U-boat, but the rocky Spanish shore was now very close as the carrier had been forced inshore by the storm.

"De Gray!" He turned, startled at the shout.

It was Guns, with CPO Drake hobbling stiffly next to him, looking pale and drawn.

"Sir?" said Guy.

Panting with the effort of moving against the fearsome wind, Guns said, "You've heard the rumours, de Gray?"

"Yessir."

"Good show. Well, the Captain has made his decision."

Guy saw Drake wipe a trembling claw of a hand across lips which were blue either from the cold or illness; he did not know which. Neither was it the time to ask such questions. Obviously, Guns hadn't come down to the gun-platform to discuss the latest buzz.

The gunnery officer's next words confirmed Guy's thoughts. "He's going to chance the storm *and* those bloody rocks inshore as well. With a neat pair of heels we might make it before the U-boat wakes up to what we're about and then we'll let the bastard have it!" he added grimly, but to Guy not totally convinced by the skipper's decision.

"But how, sir?" Guy objected, "The U-boat's not going to surface, is she?"

"Of course not," Guns said and bit his bottom lip with worry for a moment. "We're going to try to launch a Swordfish. The water's quite shallow here and the Captain is hoping that the pilot will spot the U-boat and let her have a couple of bombs before she can launch her tin-fish. Yes, I know," he added, "it'll be all very dodgy, but it's the only way." He was now business-like again.

"All right, de Gray, close up your guns and the moment the sub or anything else for that matter surfaces knock the living daylights out of it. Carry on!" Then Guns was away, following the life-line leading to the bridgehouse.

"Tall order, Chiefie," Guy commented and the flight-deck started to come to life as the Swordfish was being prepared for a very hazardous take-off.

"Yessir, but the skipper knows what he's about," the old CPO's voice was loyal but weak and quavering. "Don't you feel right, Chiefie?" asked de Gray, noting for the first time just how old Drake looked. The old fellow ought to be at home in front of a big fire, toasting his feet and enjoying a cup of tea instead of being out in this storm with his life in the balance.

"If them Hostilities Only blokes can do it, sir, poor excuses for matelots that they are, then I can, sir. I ain't that old, you know," and he forced a craggy-faced smile as proof.

"Of course you're not, Chiefie," Guy heard himself saying. "You'll live to be a hundred — see us all off, no doubt! Come on!"

As they fought their way down to the platform, Drake wished the boy hadn't said those last words. He had always seemed to have survived when younger and perhaps better men had died violently in action. It had not been fair. He hoped that this time it would be his turn, with his gammy knees and bent back. As Maggie had said often enough when he had tried to get her into bed, "You've had yer share, Duggie!"

Yes, he had.

"Stand by, engine-room!" von der Weide ordered, all hesitation gone. He raised the periscope above the heaving waves and turned on the intensifier. Suddenly, there it was — the aircraft carrier. The ship seemed to fill the whole field of view as it rolled from side to side in the heaving sea, as if the helmsman was drunk. Von der Weide took a quick look along the length of the *Ark Royal's* port side. Nothing. Nobody had spotted him so far as he could tell.

Then up on the flight-deck he caught a glimpse of red flame and he realised that the fools of Tommies were trying to launch an aircraft. He knew why, but it didn't matter now, because in a few minutes it would be all over and he and U-81 would go down in the history of World War Two.

The skipper took out his little bottle of '4711' and splashed himself with the eau de cologne to take away the stink of the U-boat and also to act as a good luck charm. Like all submariners he believed in such things and as the aroma reached his nose he immediately felt better and more confident.

"Engine-room," he called, "prepare to give me all the power you have; bow torpedo-men, close up for action." He flashed one last look round the submarine and stared into the frightened eyes of his second-in-command as he ordered, "Take her up!"

As U-81 broke the surface she was hidden in the protection of the troughs.

He used the ranging periscope: *"One thousand,"* he called, *"closing at 700 ... prepare to fire one to four ... close-up stern tubes."* The orders came from his salt-soaked lips as if he were back on some pre-war training exercise in the Baltic. He felt no tension, no fear, nothing but excitement.

This was it. Without raising his voice he commanded "Fire one to four ... *FIRE!"*

The U-boat shuddered as with an audible thump and hiss of escaping compressed air the first torpedo left the tube in a cloud of bubbles, its electric motor starting immediately and setting it speeding on its way to its target.

Von der Weide's second-in-command concentrated on his stop-watch to time the run, with the other tin-fish following in quick succession.

The skipper's eyes were glued to the rubber cap of the eye-piece on the periscope and listened to the other officer counting off the running seconds, "Fifteen ... twenty ... twenty-five ... thirty ..." Would the thing never strike home? Von der Weide cursed impatiently as he watched the carrier steam majestically on totally unaware of what must happen in a few seconds.

Then as he watched, the horizon erupted in a huge flash, a gout of flame and seconds later U-81 rocked as the shockwaves reached her. The skipper heard his second-in-command yell in triumph, "A hit ... a SHITTING HIT, sir!"

"Starboard 30," the *Ark Royal's* captain cried urgently, adding, "Make smoke!"

He never finished the order. Something wrenched him from the voice-pipe and he was flung to the deck of the bridge as *Ark Royal* suffered a terrible blow, followed by a vivid flash which blinded him for a moment. The Captain groggily climbed to his feet, deafened and feeling slightly sick and stared at the huge hole that had appeared almost at his feet. By the splintered deck was Guns, lying sprawled out in the grotesque pose of one suddenly done to violent death and the skipper, retching at the sight, noticed that the officer's head had rolled into the scuppers, leaving a scarlet trail of blood and brains behind it.

Both Guy and Drake suspected that the U-boat had fired her torpedoes while on the surface and were scanning the sea looking for it while awaiting the order to open fire. Then Guy took his eyes off the mountainous waves for a moment and looked in horror at the destruction that had been created in the split second of the torpedo hit. There was a huge hole in the flight-deck just behind the amidships elevator and from it belched livid flame and thick oily smoke.

Everywhere there were badly burned sailors, their skin hanging in strands, wandering wildly in circles, some, blinded, with hands outstretched, others crying and screaming in pain and terror. Fire-fighter crews in gasmasks and carrying extinguishers were pushing forward, heads down as if against a gale, attempting to deal with the blaze. It was agonisingly clear: the *Ark Royal* had been grievously hit. Her time was running out fast.

Up on the debris-littered bridge, with the dead sprawled everywhere in pools of their own blood, and all about them were the flames of the burning superstructure, the captain of Marines was saying urgently, "I don't think we've got much time left, sir. I've got a line rigged from the far end of the bridge. Not too difficult for you. I suggest you abandon ship now while you've still got a chance." He looked almost pleadingly at the ashen-faced Captain.

But the skipper chose to overlook the Marine's pleading. Instead, he said, "Pray have Abandon Ship sounded. At the double, Captain!" and waved his hand in dismissal. For a moment it seemed as if the Marine might refuse, then he turned and made his way off the bridge, his boots crunching over shattered glass.

CPO Drake shook his head, for he had the curious impression of a previous ship at Jutland, in 1916, sinking under him. He remembered names and faces he had long forgotten for 25 years and it was as if it were happening again, hearing the shrieks, the cries for help, the crash of collapsing decks and grinding din of falling machinery — the sounds of a ship going down.

"You all right, sir?" he called to Guy, who was leaning against the shield of a damaged quick-firer, its barrel twisted. The young officer was bleeding from a cut in his forehead.

"Yes ... yes, thanks, Chiefie!" Guy pulled himself together, forgetting the pain of his wound. "They've just sounded Abandon Ship. Give me a hand to get the chaps off, wounded first of course."

"You get to the boats first and I'll bring up the rear," Drake answered, knowing anyway that there was no chance of him getting down the scrambler-nets with those legs of his, they were too stiff. He would only endanger the rest of the draft, they were young and must have the first chance of being saved.

"No, Chiefie. We'll do both together!"

"With respect, sir — don't be a daft bugger!" yelled Drake. facing up to the astounded officer.

"Whaaaat!" gasped Guy, "What did you call me?"

"You heard me, sir. I've had my day, you're young —"

Then a shout broke into the argument. "Torpedoes!"

It was Bunts, yelling frantically and, pushing aside the dead or dying body of his friend Sparks, he depressed the elevator pedal of an undamaged Oerlikon and the cannon pounded away madly at nearly 500 rounds a minute, the red and white 20 mm tracer zipping through the air towards the lines of bubbles released by the U-81's aft torpedo tubes. But it was too late. "Hit the deck!" shrieked Drake and he dropped to the deck as the first of the tin-fish exploded against the carrier's hull directly below the gun-platform.

Guy de Gray was just a split second too late and the blast threw him off his feet, while the air was full of the acrid stink of cordite, with white-hot shrapnel lashing the air on all sides. Then he screamed with pain as what felt like a huge club smashed into his legs and he felt the bones snap and splinter as he lay, the blood jetting out of his wounds in a scarlet arc as he screamed "Oh, God! I'm dying! ... I'm..."

For a terrible moment, Drake stared appalled at the sight of so much carnage, the dead piled one upon the other, their blood mixing and steaming as if it were an abattoir. Then he pulled himself together. "I'm coming!" he quavered in a voice he did not recognise as his own, "Hang on, lads!"

The second Swordfish swooped, catching the look-outs in the conning-tower of the U-81 completely by surprise. One second the sky was empty, they had been mesmerised by the sight of the great carrier sinking, with thick black smoke trailing from her; the next second the German on the twin MGs was firing his 1000 rpm of tracer at the biplane heading straight for the submarine.

Von der Weide instinctively threw up his arms as if to ward off the attack. But the Swordfish pilot was already dead in his shattered cockpit, no longer in control and the aircraft slammed straight into the U-81's conning-tower, its petrol tank igniting and smothering the U-boat in lethal flames.

A few lived, but could never forget the worst sight of their lives as their shipmates burnt alive, human torches trying in vain to beat the flames out, thrashing in their agony. Some flung themselves into the sea, but that too was on fire and their blackened, twisted bodies bobbed up and down until they sank out of sight.

Von der Weide, the fire searing his thin body, desperately threw himself off the bridge, then he shrieked with pain as the salt-water covered his raw flesh. His body contorted, a cry was ripped from his throat and he disappeared below the waves. Then the U-81, the ship of death, began to fill with water and follow her dead skipper down to the sea-bed, carrying most of her crew with her.

It was like climbing the face of a steep, slippery mountain. The *Ark Royal* was listing to port at an ever increasing angle. Desperately, a frantic CPO Drake scrabbled up the steeply tilting deck, ducking his head as the debris of war rained down on him. He was doggedly pulling himself upward to reach the 'boy', as he had always called Guy to himself. He had known de Gray no more than a few weeks, but looked upon him as if he were his own son.

Drake squirmed up the sloping deck toward the dead body of Sparks, the face a black, encrusted, eyeless mask. "Poor bastard!" Duggie gasped, as the body slid past him down the angled deck. But he concentrated on reaching Guy as all about him sailors scrambled for the life-rafts and floats.

On the remains of the bridge-house, high above, the Captain stood alone and silent. His face revealed nothing. He could see that the gallant petty officer's attempt was doomed to failure. Then the *Ark Royal* gave a dramatic convulsion, every plate, girder, stanchion, seemed suddenly to be under unbearable pressure, its metal screaming as if a live thing about to die.

"No!" CPO Drake cried desperately, staring with a kind of longing as he saw the dead body of the young Guy de Gray above him on the sloping deck, "No! ... *Please! ...NO!"*

It was too late now. There was another violent lurch and CPO Drake began to slip backwards. He tried to hold on, but could not and lost his grip. Out of the corner of his eye he saw the Captain raise his hand to his immaculate cap in one final farewell salute as the *Ark Royal* began her last dive. Then the boilers exploded in a sheet of vivid flame and huge clouds of steam enveloped everything. It was 14 November 1941.

Then Duggie Drake lost his hold and he began to fall to the sea far below.

Afterword

From *The Navy News,* Portsmouth, May 15, 1947:

'This month we have lost an outstanding shipmate in ex-CPO Douglas 'Duggie' Drake, DCM, MBE, one of the few survivors of the tragic sinking of HMS *Ark Royal* back in November 1941.

No one knew exactly how old Duggie was. For some matelots he seemed timeless. His naval records were lost on the *Luftwaffe* attacks on Plymouth and Portsmouth in 1941. One thing is certain, however, Duggie served several lifetimes in the Royal Navy, being wounded at the Battle of Jutland in 1916 and fighting right through the Second World War, last seeing action at the landing at Walcheren in the autumn of 1944, when he won his DCM. Rumours had it that he even tried to go to the Falklands, when he must have been well into his seventies.

Even after his discharge, Duggie was a well-known figure in local naval circles and not only as a long-standing member of the Royal Naval Association. Right up to the very end he could still be seen on the Hard, erect and fierce-faced as if he were out on shore patrol on the lookout for drunken or sloppy matelots. But beneath that awesome exterior there was a heart of gold. He always had time for a young matelot down on his luck, good for a free pint and much more free good advice. Then he would let what was left of his hair down and entertain some green recruit with his tales of adventure on the high seas going back almost to the turn of the century. As his only relative, also CPO Drake, a veteran of the Falklands himself, told the local press on the occasion of his uncle's tragic death, "My uncle lived for the Royal Navy and he used to say, 'I've been blessed with the right name for it — Drake'!"

Last week, Duggie Drake met his end still fighting like his illustrious forebear, tackling a bunch of young thugs trying to rob a terrified twelve-year-old Sea Cadet on the Hard. He died, as he had lived, in action, with his blood roused, defending the honour of his beloved Royal Navy to the very end.'

THE END

35257108R00101

Printed in Poland
by Amazon Fulfillment
Poland Sp. z o.o., Wrocław